BLIND TRUST

BROTHERHOOD PROTECTORS WORLD

DEBRA PARMLEY

Twisted Page Press LLC

BROTHERHOOD PROTECTORS

ORIGINAL SERIES BY ELLE JAMES

Dedicated to Elle James, for your friendship through the years, for publishing my books, especially the ones dear to my heart set at Three C's ranch, and for your support and encouragement. Love you bunches.

ACKNOWLEDGMENTS

Thank you to Elle James and Twisted Pages Press. Thank you to Sheri L. McGathy for the gorgeous cover. Thank you to Delilah Devlin for editing. Thank you to my PA and sister, Kimberly Lear, for your hard work all year and for your love, support and encouragement. Thank you to Charles "Tazz" Welshan's for advice on San Diego, Marines, action adventure capture and fight scenes and for many years of advice and encouragement. To all the guys at White Rabbit Protection, thanks for the classes and hands on knife exercises.

To Michael Parmley, my husband and patron of the arts these many years, now cook, beta reader, plot advisor and first editor. There are so many things large and small that you do to help me throughout the year, I could never list them all. I Love you.

Thank you to my readers and reviewers, for reading, reviewing and telling others about my books. We are a symbiotic circle and I appreciate you more than I can say.

I love you all.

CHAPTER 1

BRIAN MENG KEN AKA "BARBIE," a veteran recon Marine, and the newest member of Brotherhood Protectors, turned to see what his boss, Hank "Montana" Patterson, was watching as they talked about the security at Three C's Ranch.

The Triple C Ranch, affectionately known as the Three C's Ranch, was one of two Three C's facilities in the United States, where women came after they had been attacked or abused. They came to learn new skills in order to move beyond simply surviving to thriving in their future lives.

Not every woman was accepted into the program. First, a doctor had to certify she was clear of alcohol and drugs and fit to travel, swim, ride horses and take self-defense classes. Her finances had to be in order, and there could be no upcoming court appearances. Once at the center, they had to stay until their time was done. If they had to leave for any reason, they couldn't return. Still, there was a waiting list.

While the centers were nonprofit organizations with generous donors, there was a sliding-fee scale based on income. Women were expected to contribute. Breaking a dependent cycle was part of the center's work with victims who'd been attacked or abused, so they were nudged out of the nest like baby birds just as soon as they appeared able to fly independently.

Unfortunately, their "nest" at the Triple C's Ranch in Montana had been attacked and was still under repair.

Hank was watching a shapely, silver-haired woman to Brian's far left, as the pretty woman walked toward a broom—directly toward it, as if she didn't see the broom.

Hank turned away from the conversation he and Brian were having and called out, "Cecelia, stop."

She stopped, turning toward Hank. At that moment, Brian realized Cecelia was blind.

Hank hurried over to her, moved the broom

out of the way, and said, "There was a broom in your direct line."

"Oh. Thank you," she replied, her voice soft, her tone relieved. "My shins have taken a real beating since all these workmen started on the repairs."

"They don't think," Hank said.

"No, they don't," she said. "One left out a ladder after he'd finished for the day, and another left extension cords all over the place. Now, a broom. I'll be glad when their work is done, and things get back to normal around here."

"I bet you will," Hank said. "Where's your cane?"

"At my desk," she said. "I was only heading to the restroom. Usually, there's nothing in my path in this direction."

Brian listened to her voice, the soft tones floating into his ears like a melody he wouldn't soon forget.

She looked too young to have silver hair, but perhaps she'd colored it that way. Straight and silky, it hung to her shoulders. Silver, sleek, and cut straight across the bottom. Touchable hair. The kind he enjoyed running his fingers through.

Brian took in the sight of her, as though she was a long drink of cool water, his slow perusal of her unhampered. She couldn't see the way he drank her in, which meant his gaze could take her in as long as he wanted. He enjoyed the journey.

She wore a pink tank top over full, rounded breasts, her tank top ending just above her belly button as the tank had bunched up. A thick brown leather belt held up faded blue jeans, which molded to her curves.

She is stunning.

"All clear ahead?" Her tone held a note of laughter now, and not an ounce of weakness.

"All clear," Hank replied. "I'll have a word with the workmen about picking up after themselves."

"No need," she replied. "I should've had my cane. The men have been told. They don't listen anyway, and besides," she shrugged, "I need to find my own way around things."

"You're an inspiration to many," Leah White Crane said, as she came down the hall toward them. The Native American woman knew the women at the ranch quite well, as she was the on-site counselor Hank had introduced Brian to before she'd been called away to her office to handle a small crisis, leaving the men standing here talking about the job.

"When women come here with an 'I can't attitude,' and see you running the front office, keeping everything straight," Leah said with a smile in her voice. "It's not long before they lose that 'can't' and begin to think 'I can.'"

"I don't do any more than another woman with my training." Cecelia said.

"Cecelia, I'd like you to meet Brian," Hank said. "He just joined Brotherhood Protectors and will be security on the night shift here at the ranch."

"Cecelia is our receptionist and secretary and lives on site," Leah said.

Brian swallowed. "Nice to meet you, Cecelia."

Cecelia moved toward him, smiling and held out her hand. "Nice to meet you as well, Brian."

"My pleasure." Brian grasped her hand in his larger hand. Her soft skin felt cool against his, as if she'd just washed her hands.

Her nostrils gave a slight flare as she inhaled, and he took in every nuance of her face. He was aware of her scent as well, and their first touch was almost electric.

As he continued to clasp her hand, he liked the way it felt, holding her hand in his. He gave it a gentle squeeze before letting go.

"Likewise," she said, her face looking up toward his with a radiant smile. She couldn't know he was three inches taller than her, though she directed her face toward the sound of his voice.

It's a shame she can't see me.

He was used to how women reacted to meeting him for the first time and the way they responded to his fitness and good looks. Even before they learned he was a Recon Marine. For the first twenty years of his life he had eaten up the attention and the comments, but being a Marine had taught him discipline and maturity and over the last few year the comments had finally grown old.

Cecelia was the first woman he'd met who'd had no reaction to how he looked. It was refreshing not to have a woman fawning over him.

And yet, while they'd held each other's hands, he'd felt something and was pretty sure she'd felt it, too. That chemical reaction of attraction wasn't dependent on sight. Pheromones were scented, drove attraction.

The ranch house they stood inside still bore the odors of the fire which had nearly destroyed the back of the building before the volunteer fire department had arrived to put it out. Workmen were here to rebuild the ranch house, the only building with fire damage, and Brotherhood Protectors were providing security until construction was completed and a good security system installed.

From what Hank had explained to Brian, when he'd hired him for the job, crazy men who'd been after one of the residents had set the Three C's Ranch on fire to smoke the woman out.

Afterward, the management back east had taken the security of the ranch more seriously and no longer assumed a remote location was enough protection for the women. From now on, the ranch would have security guards and cameras.

Brian was one of four men who would work security shifts, rotating days and nights to make sure the residents were protected during the build.

He'd be introduced to all the female residents and staff, so they'd know him and be comfortable with his presence when he roamed the grounds at night.

Outside the main building of the Three C's Ranch lay several charred log timbers from the lodge, which had been removed. Brian had seen them as they drove up to the ranch. Reconstruction of the lodge would be completed by next month.

Brian watched Cecelia walk to her desk and then settle in, fascinated by the way the pretty woman found her way. Once her hand was on the chair it, appeared she knew just where everything was located.

CECELIA WENT BACK to her desk and put on her headset again, increasing the volume. The noisy workers were at it again, she could hear them, even with her headset on—every single sound they made, sawing and hammering, and the popping of their nail guns. She'd been getting headaches from all the noises, and it had been making it hard for her to do her job well.

She answered a call and tried to forget about the man she'd just been introduced to, whose voice had made her stomach flutter and whose touch gave her tingles and warmth all at once.

Her hand still felt the remnants of his touch, and she could still smell his scent, which was clean and nicely male. Not every male had a good scent. His made her want to draw closer. He was still much on her mind, even though she was trying hard to focus on her job.

One thing she prided herself on was doing her job well.

"Hold just a minute please," she said, to the

young woman on the line. Placing the call on hold, she reached for the braille keyboard attached to her computer, typed in 'oral surgeons' and did a search for the closest ones in the area, using a program for the blind, which read information from any website on the internet.

The young woman wanted to come to the ranch and go through the program, but she'd just been told she needed to have all four wisdom teeth removed. So, she was worried she'd lose her spot and have to wait again to be let in. With only two centers in the U.S., the wait list could be long, even once a woman jumped through all the hoops to qualify.

It wasn't unusual for one of the women scheduled to come to the ranch to need some kind of medical care, but this was the first one who'd needed oral surgery.

Feeling the braille keyboard, Cecelia saved the information to her list of medical and dental contacts, and then picked up the call again.

"Yes, there are a couple of dental surgeons to choose from. You'll have to go to Bozeman, Montana to have any dental surgery done. One of us would drive you there and back. You wouldn't be alone, and we would make sure one of us was able to look after you while you recovered here."

Cecelia loved this part of her job. Making things better for the women and helping them step into a better future for themselves, one in which they were empowered, gave her great satisfaction.

If asked what she liked about her job, she would have said, putting things together, making plans for the ladies and keeping everything running smoothly. There wasn't anything about her job she didn't love.

BRIAN HAD BEEN WORKING security at the ranch for over a week when he asked Cecelia out. He waited until it was break time and she'd gone into the ranch kitchen for a glass of lemonade and an oatmeal raisin cookie.

She looked up at him as he entered the room. "Would you like a cookie, Brian?" she asked.

Somehow, she always seemed to know when he entered the room, despite the quiet way he moved.

"How do you always know it's me?" he asked.

"Your scent," she said. "It's unique."

"In a good way, I hope," he drawled.

"Oh, yes," she said. "A very good way." She smiled and held the plate of cookies out to him.

"Thanks," he said. "They look delicious."

"Lemonade?"

"I'm not much into lemonade," he said.

"Milk then," she said. "Cookies are always good with milk." She laid her cookie down and moved toward the fridge.

"I can get it," he said. "Go on and enjoy your cookie. You don't need to wait on me."

"Okay." She gave in with no argument and moved back to her own cookie to take another bite.

He went to the fridge, removed the milk, and then found a glass to pour it in.

"Emma makes the best cookies," Cecelia said.

"She does," he agreed. "I could get spoiled, working here."

"I'll bet you don't get many cookies on your jobs," she said.

"This is the first job I've had where I've received even one cookie," he said, with a laugh. "My jobs have been chasing down bad guys, or guarding somebody, or something."

"What, they never handed out cookies? As a

reward?" She laughed. "Someone needs to renegotiate your compensation."

"The bonuses were good. No cookies though." He dunked his cookie into the glass of milk and took a bite.

"Her oatmeal raisin cookies are my favorite," she said.

"They are really good," he said, still munching on a bite.

When they'd finished the cookies, he seized the moment. "This has been fun," he said.

"It has," she agreed.

"Let's do this again," he said. "How about dinner in Bozeman this weekend?"

"You don't want to go out with a blind girl," she said, shaking her head.

"Yes, I do," he said. "But not with just any blind girl. I want to go out with *you*."

She laughed. "I'm nothing special. And anyway, I don't date, I don't do friends with benefits, and I'm done with relationships. But even if I did date, a relationship with me would be a lot of work. Men don't handle that well."

"I'm a Marine," he said. "We're used to a lot of work, overcoming obstacles, and succeeding at our goals."

"Maybe so, but I'm not ready to go out," she said. "I'm safe here, and I know where everything is."

"You'd be safe with me, and I'd make sure you knew where things are," he said.

"You're going to keep trying to convince me, aren't you?" She tilted her head toward him, looking upward, with an exasperated look on her face.

"Yes, ma'am, I am." He nodded, then caught himself, realizing she wouldn't see him nod. "What will it take to get you to say yes?"

"You don't understand." She shook her head. "I'm not going to get my sight back. This is how things will always be. And I don't date. You should just give up now."

"Give up?" He laughed. "You're trying to convince a Marine to give up? Now *that* is funny."

Cecelia paused, thinking. Then she laughed. " I guess it is."

The real reason she wouldn't go out, the one she wasn't about to tell him, was that she was afraid to go out on a date with another man, any man she didn't know well, who might turn violent.

That crazy Elijah Blair, whom she'd gone out with, had turned violent, and back then, she could see.

They'd gone out. But he'd behaved so strangely, she'd turned him down for a second date. Yet even with full sight, she still hadn't seen the attack coming. When he'd come at her with a baseball bat, she'd had no clue.

Now, she was even more vulnerable, completely unable to see an attack coming at her. She would miss those microseconds if a crazy man flipped that switch, and she'd never see it on his face.

No way am I dating anyone. The risk is too great. If I'd been blind when Elijah swung that baseball bat, I'd have been dead. I can't risk dating anyone.

However, she didn't say any of that. She ignored the way his voice reached something deep inside her, and the way his scent made her want to lean in, closer to him. Instead, she just shook her head, picked up her cane, and stretching it out before her, walked away.

CHAPTER 2

BRIAN STOOD QUIET, watching her move down the hall, and then he turned and headed out to his car. He needed to go for a drive and think about what it might take to get her to say yes.

He was outside, opening the door of his mustang, when Leah strode toward him.

"I overheard your conversation with Cecelia and wanted to catch you before you left." Leah gave a slight frown. "It won't be easy getting Cecelia to go out on a date with you, away from the ranch, but I do think it would be good for her. However, you should know what she's dealing with. I can't divulge what she's told me in counseling, you'll have to talk to her to learn more than I tell you today. Just know there's an issue she needs to work through and don't take her rejection personally."

Concern over what might be keeping Cecelia from saying yes now entered his mind, along with questions of what it might be. The Three C's Ranch did harbor abused women. "Thanks," Brian said. "Any input you have, I appreciate."

Leah tilted her head as she locked her gaze with his. "Has she told you what caused her blindness?"

"No," he shook his head. "But I'm hoping we'll get to that topic soon."

"She was attacked savagely outside a mall in Detroit," she said. "Her attacker went after her with a baseball bat."

"Dammit," he bit out.

"The injuries are what caused her blindness. Two years ago, it was on all the news stations at the time. Elijah Blair. I'm surprised you didn't hear about the attack."

"I was probably overseas when it happened," he said. "The timeframe is right."

"It was all over the news," she said. "Everyone talking about the 'Batter Up' attacker."

"Much of the time, I wasn't getting the news over in the Middle East," he said.

"I'd rather you hear what happened from her or

from me," Leah said. "There has been gossip among the women, which I had to put a stop to. They don't realize how keen her hearing is, or how soft her feelings are, especially when they start talking about what happened to her."

"People who gossip don't care," he said. He hated that anyone had been gossiping about her. She seemed to be a sweet woman and deserved to be treated better than that.

"As for the rest of her story," Leah continued, "she's finally been able to tell it in small groups, and last month we recorded her on video, sharing her story, so it could be shared with our other center and with the ladies here. We have a collection of videos of the resident's stories, only to be shared within the centers, to help new residents understand that they are far from being in this alone, and that other women have gone on to thrive after participating in the program."

"That's great," he said. "I'm glad she's grown stronger."

"You're new, and normally I'd tell you to give this more time, but your interest in her is clear, and I don't want to put this off," Leah said. "Since her story is out publicly enough that most everyone here on the property knows it, I can tell you this much: Cecelia went on a first date with a man she barely knew, and when she turned him down for sex, and then turned him down for a second date, he stalked her to the mall, the following night and took along his baseball bat. Elijah Blair owned several Blair's Batter Up batting ranges and practiced often. When she turned him down, something made the man snap, and she was the recipient of his rage. He followed her to that mall and in the parking lot, went after her with that bat."

Brian clenched his fists as anger filled his body with each word she spoke. The desire to kill the man who'd harmed Cecelia fueled that anger.

"He nearly killed her," Leah said. "She was lucky he didn't, but her face and skull were fractured during the attack, which left her with bleeding on the brain and permanent damage to her optical nerves."

"Damn." He frowned. "I hate that she went through that."

"I do, too," she said. "But she has healed physically to the extent she will heal, and now she has to wrangle the emotional aspects of her recovery. You can help. There aren't many men who come here, for her to talk to."

"She's amazing," he said. The beautiful woman he was attracted to had survived more than many veterans he knew.

"She is," Leah said.

"Where's the guy now?"

"Behind bars for a very long time," she said, her gaze hardening.

"Not in for life?"

"The prosecutor was new." She shook her head. "And not a good one."

Brian watched Leah's face as she spoke, keeping his thoughts to himself. Thoughts of what he could do to the man filled his mind. The guy was lucky to be behind bars.

Leah studied his face as well, no doubt using her therapist's skills, and likely reading his emotions. He knew he had to keep his temper under control. He could manage that. He wasn't one to do something stupid.

The past was nothing he had any control over. What he could do was protect Cecelia now, and in the future, to make sure no one else hurt her. And that was a job he would take very seriously.

Hearing her story had brought out his protective instincts.

"The best thing you can do for Cecelia now,"

Leah said, "is to understand where she's coming from. She has fears about going beyond the boundaries of the ranch and has deep fears about going on a date. It's not about *you*; it's about going on a date with *anyone*. And her PTSD may kick in if you do convince her. The recent arson attack on the ranch house hasn't helped things. She needs someone to talk to besides me. She needs a friend."

He nodded, listening. "We can start out being friends," he said. "But I'm still going to keep asking her out."

"Good." Leah nodded. "That will boost her self-esteem. Just don't push her too hard. Keep it light."

"Will do," he said.

So, Cecelia's afraid to go out on a date? Then we won't go 'out'. We'll go in.

If he couldn't get her to go out on a date to a place away from the ranch, then he'd have to date her here at the ranch.

There was more than one way to woo a woman.

He'd go slow, and she'd learn she could trust him.

Trust had to be earned, and that took time.

THE FOLLOWING WEEK, Brian walked into the ranch house carrying his lunch. Cecelia could always tell it was Brian when he entered the room, because he smelled so good.

Today the scents she was picking up on were Brian and something yummy, likely a sandwich.

Her stomach growled, and she realized she was hungry though it was only eleven o'clock. Early for her to eat lunch and early for him to be here.

"Hello, Brian," she said, with a smile. "You're early today."

"How did you know it was me?" he asked as he stepped over to Cecelia's desk, holding his lunch.

"By your scent," she said, her smile deepening. She was not about to tell him how good he smelled.

"Again with the scent. You're like a blood-hound," he said. "You always know when I am near."

"A little," she said and laughed.

"How are you today?" he asked, his tone deepening.

"Fine," she said, shivering a little because she liked the sexy edge to his voice. "Something smells good." She smiled up at him. "Lunch?"

"Italian sub," he said, holding a bag from the

deli, which held the long Italian sub and a bag of barbeque chips. "Do you like subs?"

"Yes," she said. "I do."

"The deli was running a lunch special, and a whole sub is more than I can eat for lunch today," he said. "Want the other half?"

"Sure," she said. "Thank you."

His grin went wide, though she couldn't see it. "When do you take your lunch?" he asked.

"Right now," she said, pushing her chair away from the desk and standing.

"Good," he said.

"I'll just tell Emma, our cook," she said. "So she'll know not to prepare anything for me."

"Does she usually fix your lunch?"

"Yes," Cecelia nodded. "I take all my meals here at the ranch. It's part of my compensation package, and I don't have to worry about shopping or cooking."

"Nice perks off the job," he said.

"Yes, Emma takes good care of me here. She's a fabulous cook. So, I lucked out."

"Yes, you did," he said. He could see how cooking might be difficult for a blind person. He couldn't imagine how they managed it.

There were a lot of things he wondered how

she managed. Since he'd met her, questions had been gathering in his mind.

"Okay, I'll go tell Emma and have her make us some lemonade or iced tea," she said. "Which would you prefer?"

"Iced tea, unsweetened."

"No sugar at all?"

"I like to add my own."

"Okay, I'll be sure she brings some sugar packets, too" she said.

"Perfect," he said.

He was glad Cecelia had agreed to share his lunch. It would give them a chance to get to know each other better. Cecelia fascinated him, and he wanted to know more about her.

"Indoors, or out?" he asked once she came back from talking with Emma.

"Out," she said. "I need the fresh air."

"You pick the spot," he said. "And I'll follow you."

"Okay," she said. She walked to the front door and onto the big wooden front porch. "This okay?" she asked.

"Sounds good," he said. He was still getting used to the fact she couldn't see his nods, or his smiles, and how all good communication with her required words.

Before meeting her, he'd never realized how much he smiled and nodded and used nonverbal communication. In his job as a Recon Marine, and now his job in security, it was essential to be able to communicate silently with his teammates.

Talking to Cecelia had opened up his world even more to seeing things from a different angle.

He realized many of the mannerly gestures he made, she would never see. She might sense them, and she was quite good at that, but she would not see them all.

But that didn't mean he would forgo them. Quite the contrary. He would need to make sure she knew he appreciated her for the lady she was, and that might mean going an extra mile or two for her.

Emma came out onto the porch, carrying one glass of iced tea and one of lemonade.

"Hello Mr. Ken," Emma Ives said, handing him his drink.

He could see he was not the only one here on this ranch who was more formal. "Hello, Mrs. Ives," he said. "You can call me Brian."

"One day, Mr. Ken," she said, nodding.

"Mrs. Ives," he nodded back at her, smiling.

"You are welcome to join us for meals, Mr. Ken," she said, reaching into her pocket and pulling out four sugar packets and placing them on the table for him. "No notice needed. Or help yourself to the welcome cookies and the evening cookies."

"Mrs. Ives," he said. "I would have to spend many more hours in the gym if I were to eat your delicious food. But thank you for the invitation."

"The kitchen's always open to you, Mr. Ken," she said. "You are always welcome."

After more head nodding and smiles, Mrs. Emily Ives went back into the kitchen.

"Wow," Cecelia said after the cook went inside. "That was like watching one of those movies about people who live in the manor houses. So mannerly. What happened to my Marine and my cook?" She laughed.

"Just being respectful," he said. "Believe it or not, a Marine can also be a gentleman. You should see our dress ball."

He froze with the words that had slipped out before he'd thought about what he was saying.

It was the most awkward moment. He couldn't imagine what she was feeling. Had he hurt her by speaking before he thought?

She laughed, making the moment pass. "So, you're not all covered with green paint and ready to slip into the jungle? I won't know what to think of you now. You'll have to tell me if it's a jungle day or a dress up day."

He wanted to hug her and give her a kiss. This sweet woman was making the moment fun and trying to make *him* feel better.

"Yes, Miss Cecelia, I certainly will. Now, since you have your lemonade, are you ready for your sandwich?"

"Oh yes," she said and held out her hands.

He opened the bag and took the sandwich out, breaking the two halves apart and handing hers to her.

They ate and chatted about the weather, who would be at the ranch this week, and when this current group of women would leave and the next group would arrive.

Then he finally decided to broach the subject he'd been wanting to talk about, to learn more about her.

She seemed relaxed now, and she'd made him feel better about his mistake earlier.

Brian knew part of the answer to his question

before he asked, because Leah had told him about what had happened to Cecelia, but he wanted Cecelia to tell him first-hand what had happened to her.

He wanted her to feel she could talk to him about anything.

"I haven't asked you," he started, softening his voice, "but I've been wondering about your blindness..." He paused, looking to see whether she stiffened, but she didn't. "What happened to you? How did you lose your sight?"

She inhaled a deep breath, held it, and then released it and spoke, "A man I went on a date with took a baseball bat to my head. My face and skull were fractured, my brain bled, and there was permanent damage to my optical nerves. My sight isn't coming back, in case you were wondering and hoping. This is my life now. I'm happy here at the ranch, where I can help other women. I'm not looking for anything else. So, you don't need to keep asking me out."

"I hate that it happened to you," Brian said, glad she couldn't see his expression, because she might read it as pity, and that wasn't what he was feeling. "Knowing this doesn't change a thing. I still want to go out with you. I'm still going to keep asking you out. So, don't expect me to quit. Quit is a four-letter word."

She sighed. "Marine," she said.

"That's me," he said. "Not a quitter."

She smiled at him and then said, "Well, I've got to get back to work."

"Of course," he said. "Thanks for having lunch with me."

"Thank you for the sandwich," she said, rising to go back in, just as Leah was coming out onto the porch, looking for her.

He rose with Cecelia, though she didn't see him. "My pleasure," he said. "We'll have to do this again, sometime."

"Yes," she said with a nod. "We will."

"There's a call for you, Cecelia," Leah said. "I put them on hold."

He watched the women go back inside, the smile never leaving Cecelia's face. He was glad to have had a hand at putting it there.

BRIAN WENT to visit Cecelia at her desk for a chat, thinking he would ask her out again, but when he got there, he saw there was a new woman joining the center who had just arrived, and Cecelia was processing her in.

He busied himself with checking the security system that had already been checked by the night shift and waited for a chance to speak to her.

"If you need anything," she said to the new resident, "You can stop by my desk or call the private line." Cecelia picked up a card with numbers written on it, as if her hand knew just where to go, having done it so many times. "You'll have a phone in your room you can use to call out. Please memorize this number, so you'll have an emergency number to call if you leave the property."

"I'm not going anywhere," the short woman with the dark pixie haircut said. "I don't even have a car here."

"Humor me, okay?" Cecelia reached into a drawer and fumbled to find the key she was looking for.

He already knew that each key had a braille code on it so she could tell one from the other. He'd watched her do this before and found the way she coped with things fascinating.

Everything about her intrigued him.

"You never know where you'll find yourself, and I'll feel better if you know this number," she said. "I like to know where all our ladies are, and I get nervous and worry if I think any of our ladies will be out of touch. This way, you won't be." She pulled out a key. "Here it is." She held the key out, smiling. "This key is yours. You're in the third room on the right."

"Thank you," the young woman said, taking the key.

"You're quite welcome," Cecelia said.

Another call came over the headset, and she took the call, giving the new woman a wave as she went back to work.

"Hazel, how are you?" Cecelia asked. "Everything going okay over at Rosewood Center this week?"

The Rosewood Center, in North Carolina, was the first of the two Courage and Confidence Centers to be established and worked similarly to the Three C's ranch. One evening, out of curiosity, he'd read the brochure about the centers which had been in the library on an end table. Now it

Brian had planned to ask Cecelia out again today, but she was busy every time he'd tried to talk to her.

Persistence though, he had that. And patience. Today however, did not seem to be his day.

"Just a minute, Hazel," Cecelia said. She turned toward Brian. "Is there anything you need right, now, Brian?"

He grinned and was tempted to answer with, *A kiss from you*, but instead he said, "Nothing that can't wait."

"Okay. Talk to you later." She went back to her call, and he went outside to walk around the grounds.

This security job mostly consisted of walking, watching, and checking. He could walk over to the stables and see what the ranch foreman was doing with the horses.

Yesterday, the foreman had told him the vet would be arriving right about now. It would be interesting watching what he would do with the animals today.

He wondered if Cecelia would consider going for a horse ride with him, if they chose a gentle animal and kept to the easy trail for beginners. He'd make sure to keep her safe from harm on a horse, or anywhere else.

The list of 'dating in' possibilities was growing.

The only question was would she say yes to any of them?

CHAPTER 3

CECELIA WAS PLEASED to hear Hazel's voice on the line. Hazel was one of her best friends.

Hazel Whitaker worked as a receptionist at the Rosewood Center, and she and Cecelia had become good friends while Cecelia had stayed there, learning braille and how to be a receptionist and secretary. After she'd taken the new job and moved to Montana to the brand-new Triple C Ranch to be the receptionist there, the women had kept in touch.

Both centers worked in a similar way. Women went to the centers to learn how to empower themselves, learning self-defense and other life skills to be safe and stronger when they left and started their new lives.

After graduating from the program, a woman who had been as terrified as a mouse after being the victim of a violent attack or a domestic abuse situation left the centers with new confidence, life skills, and strength.

This was certainly true for Cecelia. Her time at Rosewood Center had been amazing. Newly blind, she'd had so many challenges. Learning to find her way around the house, the sidewalk, the grocery, the sand dunes behind the house and the ocean beyond.

She had never been terrified of the ocean before. It had taken the love and support of all her house sisters before she would even put one foot in the water.

And moving through the dunes? Another major hurdle for her.

With the support of her housemates, she'd overcome that hurdle as well. They had become as close as sisters. They all stayed in touch via email, but a phone call was a special treat.

Sometimes, working together in the same company, though at different locations, she and Hazel got to talk on company time. They always managed to catch up a little on personal matters.

Much as she enjoyed chatting with Brian, he

wasn't going anywhere. In fact, he would be here tomorrow and the next day, doing his job.

Hazel, though… Talking to her was a real, once in a while, treat.

Cecelia leaned back in her chair, enjoying the call and forgot all about Brian.

THE DREAM BROUGHT it all back as the night of the fire replayed in her mind…

The sound of gunfire woke Cecelia at once.

She reached for her braille phone on her night-stand and dialed the sheriff.

"Hello, please hurry, there's been a gunshot at Three C's Ranch. I don't know what's going on. I was asleep, and it woke me. Please hurry," she repeated.

The dispatcher on the other end of the phone told her to leave the line open, so they could hear what was happening.

She left the phone open on the nightstand and moved to the closed bedroom door. Placing her hand on the door so she'd feel anyone trying to open the door, she waited, listening.

Nothing.

The house was silent again.

She turned the doorknob and opened the door, stepping out.

Someone was in the hallway. She sensed the person before she even asked, "What's happening?"

She reached out, her hand finding a man's hairy forearm. Her hand closed around the man's arm.

He quickly pulled Cecelia out of the doorway into the hall and moved her behind him. "Put your hand on my back."

Hank Patterson. She knew his voice.

His hand was trying to move her hand to his back. She should have let him guide her.

Hank was the head of the Brotherhood Protectors. She knew and trusted him. But she was frozen with fear, standing still, listening. Sniffing.

Then she smelled it.

Fire.

Fear filled her.

She couldn't see the fire to escape it; she'd have to rely on the others to help her reach safety.

It's not safe here.

The dreams always took her back to this place. Where she stood frightened and frozen in place, unable to run and not knowing which way to run, but feeling inside like she very much needed to run to stay alive.

Then she woke.

She still had nightmares about fires and not being able to get out of the building.

Tonight, she'd had another one.

Leah had reassured her the nightmares would happen less frequently with time.

Cecelia knew she was perfectly safe here now. During her waking hours everything was fine.

Leah had also reminded her, that even when those arsonists had set the building on fire, she'd still been safe.

Everyone had looked out for each other and made sure they all got out. During her waking hours, she knew all this, but it hadn't stopped her nightmares.

Fear of fire, when you've actually lived through one, is a very palpable thing. A very real thing. It wakes you with your heart racing.

And you couldn't tell yourself that a fire would never happen to you, as the real event proved that indeed, it could, and it had.

That was the monster she fought now.

She bunched up her pillow, punched it once,

and then settled down and tried to fall asleep again.

BRIAN CAME AROUND THE CORNER, just in time to hear Cecelia talking to Leah.

"There are no direct flights to San Diego from Bozeman, Montana," Cecelia said. "So now, I don't know what to do."

"You need to go to San Diego?" Brian interrupted their conversation.

If she needed to go to San Diego, he could help.

"Yes, my cousin Samantha Whitaker is in the hospital there, getting ready to have her appendix out and I need to go see her," she said.

"I just happen to be driving to San Diego tomorrow," he said.

"You're kidding," she said.

"Nope. Serious as hell. One of the other guys is filling in for me tomorrow and until I'm back. I have to take care of some things on base," he said. "I plan to drive. You can ride along."

"That's a long way to ride along," she said.

"Yep. It's an eighteen-hour drive to San Diego from here. I could make it in two days, but for the two of us, I'll make it three. So, you won't be on the road more than six hours a day and can rest. And I'd enjoy the company."

He watched Cecelia's face as she considered his offer, one little wrinkle line winding across her forehead. A worry line.

"This will solve your problem, and I've already been vetted to protect you and escort you," he said. "As good as a hired bodyguard. Better, since you know me."

"He's right, you know," Leah said. "If we hired you an escort, Brian is the man they'd send. Or someone like him. You have nothing to fear with him escorting you."

"Okay, okay," Cecelia said, putting her hands up in surrender. "Enough persuading. I can't take both of you pushing me. I'll ride along to San Diego. Sam said San Diego is rougher than it used to be. She wasn't keen on me coming out alone."

"Great," Brian said. "I'm looking forward to our trip."

"I am, too," she said. "Thank you for taking me all the way out there to see my friend."

"You're welcome," he said. His phone beeped and looking down at it, he said, "I need to take this," and then walked outside.

As he walked, he held back a fist pump in the air that he felt like making.

Hot damn. I just wanted one date out with her, away from the ranch. Now I'll have a whole week. Plenty of time for us to get to know each other better.

CECELIA HEARD him go out the door and sighed.

What have I just agreed to? Six days on the road with Brian. I don't know if I can do this. And we have to leave tomorrow!

Fortunately, her workday got so busy she didn't have time to think on it further. She'd agreed to go, this would help them both, and now she needed to stay busy today instead of worrying about it and turning into a nervous wreck.

THE NEXT DAY, everything had been prepared, and Brian was more than ready. The gas tank on his truck was full, and he'd even washed the truck inside and out before driving to the ranch to get Cecelia. There was a cooler of water in the back, along with trail mix and apples for snacks to tide them over in between stops. He even had a solid chocolate bar in the cooler in case she got a craving for chocolate. He wanted everything about this trip to be a good experience for her.

Everything had been well planned, the way he liked things. He would stay at the Naval base while Cecelia would stay at her cousin Samantha Whitaker's house. They would need to pick up Sam's house key at the hospital when they went to see her, so the first thing they would do is visit her cousin.

Then he'd drop Cecelia off the next morning for a longer visit, while he went to his appointment on base. After which, he would come back to the hospital and take her out to lunch. She would have one more day to visit her cousin, and then they'd start the three-day drive back.

That gave him eight days together with her, to prove he was just the boyfriend she needed.

He wondered how Cecelia would handle staying alone in her cousin's house where she would be alone. If she would be afraid. But she'd explained, it was originally her aunt's house, and her cousin had inherited it. She'd spent many holidays there and was familiar with the house.

Brian could not wait to get on the road with her.

He pulled up to the ranch, parked, and got out.

Her suitcases were sitting on the big wooden porch beside the front door, and she sat in a rocking chair waiting for him. Pretty as a picture with her soft blue T-shirt and blue jeans, white socks and white tennis shoes, and her dark sunglasses on, she could have been on the cover of a magazine, promoting the restful beauty of the ranch.

Hurrying toward her and up the steps, he called out, "Good morning! Are you all packed and ready to go?"

"I am," she said, and nodded with a smile as she reached for her cane and stood.

"Good," he said. "I'm looking forward to our trip. Weather reports are good, so we should have smooth sailing."

She smiled at that. "You Marines and the sailing," she said. "It must be something, sailing on those big carriers."

"It is," he agreed. Then he changed the subject. "Stay put while I put your bags in the truck, and then I'll come back and- "

"I don't need help down the steps," she said, interrupting him, her tongue quick to respond. "I know these steps. And you need to know the ground rules before we leave. Lead a blind person only after they accept your offer to do so. Don't assume I am helpless and leap up every time. I will get around quite well, without you, most of the time."

He'd never heard her be snappish before, but she sure was this morning.

What had set her off?

"I have something for you," he said. "And I would like to give it to you here, before we get into the truck. If that is all right with you."

"For me?" Her voice held surprise. "You didn't have to get anything for me."

I might as well give it to her now, reframe this morning, and soften her mood if I can.

"Hold out your hand." His commanding voice told her not to argue with him.

She held out her hand, palm up, and waited.

He placed the purple velvet bag into her palm.

"What's this?" she asked, feeling the soft draw-string bag with the necklace inside, her fingers caressing it.

He'd picked out velvet for the texture and enjoyed watching her face as she felt the bag. Her expression had moved to one of surprise, and now, of joy. That was the look he liked to see on her, and he was glad he'd helped to improve her mood.

Her index finger moved inside the bag, opening the drawstring, and she found the necklace, hooking the chain on her finger and drawing the delicate gold chain out.

Watching her, as always, was fascinating.

"Oh," she said. "A necklace. What a nice surprise."

"It is a necklace. The chain and the pendant are gold, and the pendant has a gold owl on it," he said.

"Ooooh," she said as she ran her fingers all over it.

"But it's also a GPS," he said. "San Diego is kind of bad in some areas, and it's a big city. With you wearing GPS tracking, if for any reason we get separated, I can find you. I hope when you wear it, you'll feel safer. All you have to do is press on the front of the pendant, and that will send a signal right to an app on my phone. Then I'll see where you are and come find you."

"Oh, how thoughtful," she said. "Thank you!"

"You're welcome," he said. "Let me put it on you."

"Oh, yes," she said. "I'd like that."

He gently took the necklace from her and unfastened the clasp.

She leaned forward for him.

Then reaching both hands around the back of her neck, he found the clasp with the other side, and connected them. The pendant part of the necklace now lay nestled between her cleavage.

She placed her hand over it, flat against her chest and said, "I won't take it off again until we're back home. That way nothing can happen where I can't let you know that I need you to come find me. It feels good." She smiled. "Lightweight, but also it's comforting, like you said."

"Good," he said, and he bent to kiss her forehead.

She gave a happy sigh, her smile deepening.

"Remember, if you need me for any reason, all you have to do is press once on the pendant," he said.

"I will." She placed her hand on his arm and looked up at him, joy written all over her face. "Thank you for such a thoughtful gift."

"You're welcome," he said, enjoying seeing her happiness. "I want you to be able to relax and enjoy our trip. Now, I'll load your bags, and you can make your way to my truck. And I'll remember to ask you if you need my help, but you must also tell me when you want it or need it. Good communication must work both directions. Deal?"

"Yes." She smiled and nodded up at him. "Deal."

He watched her move her cane in front of her, and he backed away to pick up both her bags and carry them down the steps.

Once her bags were in his truck and she was to the bottom of the steps, he called, "Over here."

She walked toward him, and he thought of how brave she was being, facing her fears by taking the leap to go on this journey with him. He would do anything he could to make sure it was an enjoyable experience.

He moved around to open the passenger door of the truck and said, "I'm going to open doors for you, and will help you into my truck and out of it, and I'm going to do that because that's what a gentleman does. So, I hope you will allow me that pleasure."

"Oh." She stopped, close to him, a look of surprise on her face as if she hadn't considered that. "Well, okay. Yes, that's nice actually."

He smiled to himself, knowing it was. He'd treat her like a lady, and he was glad he wouldn't have to argue with her about it. Because it was about respect for her, not about whether she was independent or not. He was glad they'd be compatible on that note. Dating women who argued about that one was no fun for him and told him quickly whether they were compatible.

He'd been raised in a Chinese-American family, where respect and good manners were important, so his woman would need to be able to fit into that world as well, if they were to be a long-term couple. It was best to figure these things out early on, so neither of them wasted time with the wrong person.

From what he'd observed of Cecelia, and what others had told him about her, she was an amazing woman he was very much interested in.

As Leah had said, he needed to take it slow. Which wasn't a problem. He would savor each moment of this trip, each small step while he wooed her and watched her face. For that privilege alone, this trip would be perfect.

After helping Cecelia into the truck, he asked if she'd had breakfast, and she said that, yes, Emma had made her such a big breakfast she'd thought maybe the cook was afraid Cecelia wouldn't be fed on this trip.

Brian laughed. "She does like to make sure

everyone gets fed, and she fusses over you like a mother hen." He laughed again. "Okay then. We can plan for a late lunch but tell me if you get hungry. I have snacks packed and water in the cooler."

"Sounds perfect," Cecelia said. As they headed out on the road, she relaxed back on her seat and tucked her hair behind her ears because a breeze blew through the open window, spreading it across her face.

"Would you like me to roll up the window up and turn the air on?" he asked.

"No, not yet," she said. "Maybe when it gets hotter. I'm so often inside on the phone that it's nice to be riding along, feeling the wind on my face."

"Well, you just let me know when you want me to roll it up," he said.

"Okay."

They listened to the radio for a while, and then he glanced over and noticed she was dozing. Her head was leaning to the side and bobbing.

He reached for a small blue pillow behind him on the back seat, and then reached across to tuck the pillow next to her head to cushion and support her head.

She snuggled into the pillow and kept on sleeping.

He couldn't believe his good luck. Here he was, driving down the highway, this beautiful woman by his side, as they headed to San Diego.

He wondered how she'd feel about walking on the beach. Then he remembered she wouldn't be able to see the sunset.

How will she feel about that?

There were so many things he would have automatically done when dating, but now he needed to put even more thought into it.

Dating her was going to be both challenging and exciting, and he looked forward to every moment of it.

The day was spent with Cecelia dozing and waking, with a thirty-minute lunch at a burger place, which was nothing special but was the only place where she could get the milkshake she craved. She'd passed on the fries and ordered onion rings, a burger, and a chocolate shake.

They spent the time talking about their high school days and places they went after a football game for late night meals and snacks. He had played football. She had been a cheerleader. Both had enjoyed high school very much.

Then they were on the road again, miles behind them and many more to go.

Cecelia dozed off again after they ate lunch, and when he woke her for a gas refill and bathroom break, he asked if she felt all right as she'd been sleeping so much.

She confessed she'd been having nightmares lately about fires. The nights of short sleep, and restless sleep when she did get it, had caught up with her.

"Then I'm glad you've been sleeping," he said. "It sounds like you needed that rest."

He was also glad she felt comfortable enough with him to fall asleep like that. That was very good.

"I'm going to suggest something, which of course you can say no to, but I think it might be better for us both. We can get one hotel room with double beds, then I'd be there to hear you if you have another one of those dreams. I can wake you."

Her expression showed surprise, or was that shock?

CHAPTER 4

BRIAN HURRIED TO GO ON, before Cecelia said no, hoping she would say yes. "We would each sleep in our own bed though, so don't be getting any ideas just yet. It's too soon in our relationship for that."

His final tone closed the door, making it clear that sex of any sort was off the table...for now.

She sat quiet for a moment, thinking, and just when he'd thought she would say no way, she said, "Yes, I think I might sleep better, if you're there to hear me in the night. Sometimes when I wake up, I'm really disoriented and think I'm back in that fire and can't get out. Leah has suggested everything she knows to suggest, but nothing stopped the nightmares yet. And I wish they would stop."

"I hope they stop too, and I hope you sleep well tonight, all through the night," he said. "If I can do anything to help with that, please let me know. I would like to help."

"Thank you," she said. "I will."

About an hour later, he pulled the truck into the parking lot of the Dusty Trail Inn.

It was an older motel, but the ratings said it was clean, and all they needed was a clean, safe place to sleep on their route. Just a quick one-night place.

They registered for one room with two double beds, instead of two rooms, and then he carried their bags inside, while she followed behind him.

Once inside the room, he said, "Claim your bed."

She moved into the room and took the bed farthest from the door, which was the one he'd have picked for her, as it put him nearest the door in case of trouble.

She'd be closer to the bathroom. Her choice also spoke of her trust. Had she picked the one near the door, he'd have known she wasn't trusting him yet. Subconsciously, she'd have wanted a route away from him, if she didn't fully trust him.

They'd begun to work out a pattern at meals, now that they'd had lunch and dinner. He would look at the restaurant and choose his seat, where he could watch the doors and be the first to see trouble looming, so he chose whichever seat protected her more.

Once he'd explained the why, and that he didn't sit with his back to the door, she had understood and complied quite easily.

As long as he didn't tell her what to do and where to sit, she seemed fine with him taking charge.

He put her suitcase near her bed, on the low table across from the foot of the bed, and then told her where the suitcase was and that she could have the bathroom first for a shower. Then he turned on the TV, sat on the bed, and tried to give her the privacy of not watching her constantly.

When she was awake, she always seemed to sense when his gaze followed her, as if she had a second sense about it. As fascinated as he was, by how she got around and did things, he didn't want to make her feel uncomfortable, so he was going to tune out with a TV show and let her settle in for the night.

She opened her suitcase, pulled out a soft pink nightgown, a white terrycloth robe and pink slippers, along with a bag of toiletries, and then went into the bathroom to shower and prepare for the evening.

Tired of the TV show he was watching, he got up and double locked the door, so they were in for the night, and then pulled out the things he needed for the evening. Gym shorts, as he didn't own pajamas. He'd forgo his normal nightly routine out of respect for her. Though she'd never know it.

He found a Jackie Chan movie, one of his favorite actors, and was laughing at the show when she came back out of the bathroom, toweling her hair.

"What are you watching?" she asked.

"Jackie Chan," he said. "Are you familiar with his movies?"

"Yes," she said. "I've watched a couple. Before I lost my sight. Now, I don't go to movies with anyone."

He watched her speculatively.

Did she want to go to movies? Or did she avoid them because she no longer enjoyed them?

She was quiet, and moving over to her bed, before taking off her robe and sliding beneath the covers.

He wasn't sure how to ask her and wanted her

evening to be pleasantly spent on good topics before she went to sleep.

Then she spoke. "I would probably enjoy going to a movie if it had good dialog and wasn't relying on the visuals. No one has ever asked me to one since I lost my sight."

"That's a shame," he said.

"It's not like I never get to hear movies anymore," she said. "I like it when we have movie nights at the ranch. It's even better than a movie theater, because I can ask a question, or someone will tell me if the actors stop talking, what is going on. Many suspense scenes for instance, I'll know by the music that something is happening, or going to happen, but I don't know what. You can't really be talking in a movie theater though, without upsetting people. And there's no rewind and replay in a movie theater."

"So, you'd enjoy curling up on the couch with popcorn to snuggle and watch a movie," he said.

"Oh, yes. I'd enjoy that very much." She nodded. "Especially the snuggling part."

"Good." He smiled and took off his shoes. "I like snuggling and watching movies at home, too."

"Don't get me wrong," she said. "Being blind doesn't mean we can't do or enjoy television, movies, or theatre. Just think of it like those old-time radio shows. We need to hear the story, and that can be just as exciting and enjoyable, if It's done well."

"That's good," he said. "I hadn't thought of radio shows."

"Oh, and books on tape. I like those, too. Though of course, I can read with my braille reader. It's nice to be able to relax and just listen."

She was chattier than he'd thought she'd be tonight. He was glad she wasn't nervous to be in the same room with him, but maybe her chattiness right now was a sign of her nerves. "Okay, I'm going to hop in the shower. You want me to leave Jackie on, or do you want the remote to find something else?"

"This is fine," she said. "I might be asleep when you come out. I took one of the pills Leah recommended to help me sleep, and it only takes twenty minutes to kick in."

"All right. I'll be quiet so I don't wake you. My alarm is set for seven thirty. I'd like us to be on the road by eight. We can get breakfast further down the road. There's a pancake house and a local coffee shop just a few miles away."

"Sounds good," she said. "Well, good night Brian."

"Good night, Cecelia."

CECELIA NESTLED INTO HER PILLOWS, sheets and blankets, feeling the melatonin start to work. Once she laid still, it wouldn't be long until she slept. She didn't know why she had been so tired on the trip today.

Am I really that behind on sleep? Must be more than I realized. And Brian is so much nicer than I realized. He's really going out of his way to make sure I'm comfortable, safe and enjoying the trip.

Why was I so hesitant to go out with him?

Not every guy is like Elijah, which I know in my head, logically, and Leah and I have gone over that enough, but the fear of dating has been a stubborn sticking thing.

Leah said give Brian a chance and just get to know him as a friend, first. Then whether I decide to go out or not, I'll have made a new friend and that's always a good thing.

All this time on the road getting to know Brian has been so nice. And he is so nice. I guess there really are nice guys out there. You just have to find one.

If he asks me out again, I think I'll say yes. It feels right to say yes. I really like him a lot.

It was her last thought before falling asleep, and she slept soundly for the first time in months, and without one bad dream.

When she woke the next morning, and realized this, it felt somewhat like a miracle.

She was in the bathroom before his alarm went off and came out just as it began to ring.

"Good morning," she said after he turned off the alarm.

She started digging in her suitcase for fresh clothes to wear today on the second day of their trip.

"Morning," he said, watching her rummage in her suitcase for something. "I didn't hear you last night. How did you sleep?"

"I slept all night long, like a baby," she said. "I feel so much better this morning. It's amazing what a good night's sleep can do."

"Good. Yes, it is," he said. "Are you done in the bathroom?"

"Yes. Go ahead." She lifted her jeans and sniffed them, and then held them out for him to see. "Any spots on these? If not, I'm wearing them again today."

"Nope, no spots." He walked past her into the bathroom and closed the door.

She'd have privacy to get dressed, and then they'd check out and get on the road. He needed coffee to catch up with her cheerfulness, but he was happy she'd slept well.

THE SECOND DAY of driving went well. The weather remained good, except for one brief, drizzling rain that didn't last more than thirty minutes, just long enough to wash the dust off the truck.

They ate lunch at a truck stop, which she'd never done before, and they shared one slice of apple pie with a scoop of vanilla ice cream.

"I know what your plan is," she said when they were back in the truck.

"What's my plan," he said, one side of his mouth curving.

"You've going to ply me with milkshakes and pie with ice cream, and all manner of sweets, so that I'll think of our days spent together as sweet ones. It's all an evil plan to tempt me with sweets until I'm besotted with you."

He laughed. "You've got me. Is it working?"

"Oh, yes," she said. "I'm just not sure I'll fit into these jeans if you keep this up."

"Well, then we'll have to work it off of you," he said.

Her eyes went wide again as she froze and got quiet.

"We could start going for a walk after dinner, before we turn in for the evening," he said. "Or when we stop for lunch."

Relief showed on her face.

Did she really think I was talking about sex right now? We haven't even kissed. She must have gone out with some real winners, not just that guy who attacked her.

He wondered what her other relationships had been like. Before the attack.

"Unless you have some other, nefarious plan to get me naked and work the sweets off," he said.

She laughed. "No, I'm not the nefarious type. No dastardly naked plans in this girl."

"Well, that's a good thing," he said. "Cause I'm not ready to get naked with you."

Surprise showed on her face. "You're not?"

"Nope. It's too soon," he said. "We're just getting to know each other. No reason to rush things."

He wished he could capture the look on her

face just then, as she sat taking in what he'd said. There were a lot of expressions he'd like to capture.

The many looks she'd shown him so far on this trip. He'd never forget them, as they'd be frozen into his memory. But for a moment, he wished he could capture this image.

He wondered how she felt about having her picture taken.

"I would like to rush into one thing, though," he said.

"You would?" she said. "What one thing?"

"Kissing," he said, smiling wryly. "I've been wanting to kiss you for weeks. But the timing needs to be right for a first kiss. At some point on this trip, after we see your friend, I'm going to kiss you—if you're all right with that."

"I'm all right with that," she said, her words rushed. "But I thought maybe you were going to ask me out again."

She sounds disappointed.

Inwardly, he wanted to shout, *Yes!* But he kept this to himself. "Does that mean you're ready for me to ask you out?" he asked instead.

"Mmm-hmm," she answered.

Joy filled his chest. "Miss Cecelia, may I have

the pleasure of taking you to dinner in San Diego, as our official first date, followed by a walk on the beach?"

"Oh, yes!" she said. "That sounds fantastic!"

Amazing, he thought. *She's gone from not wanting to go out at all to enthusiasm and a yes.*

And that was perfect.

"It will be," he said. "It's a date."

Now, they had two more nights to anticipate their official romantic date. Everything about this trip was going perfect. He almost couldn't believe it was going so well.

He'd thought convincing her would be a lot harder.

They reached the next hotel later than he'd planned. The only room available for them was a room with a king-sized bed on the second floor.

Not what he had planned, at all.

CECELIA COULD HEAR the frustration in his voice as he tried to get them another room.

There was some kind of event in town, and all the local hotels were full.

He'd started to argue with the front desk clerk, when Cecelia reached for his arm and tugged to get his attention. "It's okay," she said. "Take the room."

"Fine," he said. Then to the desk clerk, he said, "Can I get a cot?"

"We don't have any left," the clerk said. "Sorry."

"We don't need one," Cecelia said. "There's no reason we can't share the king." She could feel his gaze upon her, though he didn't say a word. She wondered what he was thinking.

He paid for the room, and then asked if there was an elevator.

There was not.

"It's fine," Cecelia said. "I can manage stairs. No biggie."

Outside, they walked to the truck.

"I'll sleep on the floor," he said.

"No, I'm not having you sleep on the floor," she said. "And I'm not going to argue with you about it. That's silly."

They stopped at the truck, and he got their bags out.

"It's not silly. It's respectful."

"No, it's silly," she said. "Unless you don't think you can keep your hands off me, if we share a king-sized bed. They're pretty big beds, you know, and I'm not a large woman. In fact, you might have trouble finding me in such a big bed. Which is why it's silly to sleep on the floor. Those beds are huge."

"I'm not going to argue with you about this," he said.

"Good, then you'll sleep on the bed," she said. "You do know I sleep on a single bed at the ranch, right? Even the queens and doubles seem big to me after my bed. Please share the king with me."

"Fine," he said.

BRIAN BEGAN TO SWEAT. She had no idea what she was asking. Sleeping in the same bed next to her, with her soft curves and sweet face, her unique scent which he found so enticing, her soft snores telling him she slept, and the way she sighed in her sleep, he'd be lucky if he got any sleep at all.

But she wanted him there, so he would do it.

"Thank you," she said. "I'll sleep better now."

I'm glad one of us will, he thought.

Too bad she can't take a turn driving. A six-hour drive won't be easy if I don't get enough sleep.

Maybe she'll share one of those melatonin pills she takes. She said they're all natural and not habit-forming, so it can't hurt to try one.

Going up the stairs was a slow process, as she found her way up by herself.

He'd have liked to have carried her up, to get her in the room faster, but he had both their suitcases in his hands, and she wouldn't have gone for him carrying her up anyway.

He realized his lack of sleep from the night before was making him impatient and cranky.

Again, he turned on the TV after they got in the room, and sat on the bed watching it, while she got her shower.

He had dozed off when she came out saying, "What's on?"

Her voice woke him. "No idea. I dozed off."

"I'm out now. The shower is all yours," she said.

"Thanks." He grabbed his clothes then went in to take his shower.

When he came out, she was awake and listening to a rerun of Johnny Carson.

"Johnny is still funny," she said. "Even when the shows are dated. I listen to comedians more than I used to. It feels good to laugh."

"It does," Brian agreed. "Johnny is good. Hey, can I try one of your melatonin's? I need a good night's sleep."

"Sure." She rose and went to get the bottle. She

picked it up then held it out to him. "They work really well."

He took the bottle from her. "Thanks."

He popped one and got into bed. He turned on his side, facing away from her. "Good night."

"Good night," she said as she got into bed, too.

He waited in silence, staying still, as he felt every movement she made, heard every sound, and imagined what touching her in this bed would be like.

She moved around in the bed, making the mattress move, as she wiggled to get comfortable.

With a huge effort, he forced his thoughts to something else. The only thing he could come up with was the date he'd plan for them once they got to San Diego and where he might take her to dinner. Then the melatonin kicked in and, as she'd said, it worked.

Tonight however, she didn't sleep all the way through. One of her nightmares woke her.

Groggy with sleep, he heard her cry out.

"Help me, there's a fire," she mumbled.

He felt her rolling in the bed like a crocodile, lost in the dream, before her hand reached out to him, landing on his belly.

His stomach muscles clenched at her sudden touch.

And then she was next to him, her soft round breasts up against him, her hand smooth on his muscled belly, and down below, his quick and hard response to her touching his bare skin wasn't something he could ignore.

He wanted her. Now.

But she was in the midst of a bad dream, so this was not the time to get horny, and then naked together.

This is not how our first time will be. She'll be fully awake and freely saying yes to sex, or we won't be having sex.

He'd known sleeping in this bed with her was a bad idea. But now, she needed him, so he held her close, and said, "Cecelia, baby, wake up. You're having a bad dream. But you're okay. You're safe."

She woke slow, groggy, yet seeming to want to burrow in against his warmth and strength, holding onto him as if that would keep her safe.

He tightened his arms around her and repeated the words, "You're okay."

When she was fully awake, her face flushed red, and she pulled away. "I'm sorry," she said. "I didn't mean to rub up against you like that."

"It's okay," he said. "I understand you were dreaming, and you were scared. And I don't mind holding you. In fact," he held open his arms, and then, remembering she couldn't see the gesture, he reached for her hand and tugged as if to pull her to him. "You can come back, come snuggle, if you want to. I'll just hold you."

"You'll just hold me?" The look she gave him was incredulous.

"Damn, baby, what kind of self-centered assholes have you been dating?" he said. "Of course, I'll just hold you. Come back over here."

With her eyes wide, she moved back into his arms.

Before she fell asleep again, her cheek against his chest, she said, "They really were assholes. Every single one."

His response was to squeeze her once, kiss the top of her forehead, and say, "Sleep now."

Within seconds, she was softly snoring.

It took him nearly another hour to fall asleep again.

In the morning, they both moved apart, and he went into the bathroom first, not wanting her to know he was aroused from holding her all night.

It had been a sweet torture for him when he

was awake, but he would have done it for her again, without hesitation. She had needed him.

When he came back out, everything was under control.

They both got ready to leave, neither mentioning the night before.

It wasn't until they'd both eaten half their omelets and drank some coffee that either of them felt like broaching the subject.

"I...," She hesitated as she spoke, looking down at her plate. "I liked sleeping in your arms last night."

Why is she looking down? There's nothing she can see on her plate. This is an emotional thing, not a sight thing. She doesn't need to look down when she talks to me.

He placed his finger under her chin and raised her face. "Hey, beautiful," he said. "I want to see your beautiful face. Don't hide from me. You can tell me anything."

She blinked, and then looked straight toward him. "I liked it. I liked it a lot."

"I liked it, too." His thumb paused on her lips. "I'm going to enjoy kissing you."

"I'm going to enjoy that as well," she said.

"So, we'll reach San Diego tonight," he said. "Are you ready?"

"Yes," she said. "I'm excited about our date."

"Me, too." He let go of her chin and lips and picked up his fork. "Eat up, we need to get going soon."

She picked up her fork. "Yes, we do."

CHAPTER 5

When they reached San Diego, they went straight to Sharp Memorial Hospital. He parked the truck in the visitors' parking lot, and they walked to the entrance.

"I can do the elevators myself," she said. "They'll have braille posted."

"Okay," he said.

Inside the hospital, he waited, letting Cecelia press the elevator button instead of doing it for her. He really had to curb his tendency to take charge and help, so she wouldn't feel like he thought she couldn't do something. But all in all, they were getting along well, and learning how to be together easily and comfortably.

As they stood waiting for it to open, he looked

at the braille near the UP button and the braille near the DOWN button. Things he'd never paid much attention to before.

Cecelia stood with a cheerful look on her face as she waited for the elevator to ding.

"Do you find most places have braille for you to read buttons or signs, or is it an issue?" he asked.

"Depends on the place," she said. "Many blind people can read braille, most do not," she said. "We're not one size fits all, so you have to ask people. Some of us use canes, some have dogs, some read braille, some do not."

Ding.

The elevator doors opened, and Cecelia moved forward, using her cane.

"I've got the door," he said, as he reached for it, to hold it open for her.

"Thank you," she said, and then she moved past him into the elevator, reaching the back then turning to face out.

After stepping inside, he pressed the fourth-floor button, and the doors closed. He stood beside her, wondering if she would be nervous about elevators if he weren't there with her.

The elevator stopped on the fourth floor, and they got out and headed down the corridor.

One of the nurses walking toward them rolled a stand with fluids for a patient.

"Excuse me," Cecelia said, as her cane bumped into the leg of the stand.

"You're fine, sweetheart," the nurse said. "Can I help you find a patient?"

"Yes. Sam Whitaker."

"She's in room 417, past the nurse's station in the corner." The nurse eyed Brian as she gave them directions.

"Thanks," he said.

"Oh, thank you," Cecelia said, sending a beaming smile in the nurse's direction.

"You're quite welcome," the nurse said, smiling in return.

Brian noted again the reaction people had to Cecelia.

Does she have any idea how often she makes others smile? How much she brightens our lives?

That was something he wanted to tell her, when the time was right.

Maybe tonight at dinner.

WHEN BRIAN PICKED Cecelia up at Sam's house, she

was wearing a sleeveless, flowered dress and sandals.

"You look beautiful," he said.

"Thank you."

"Just one little thing," he said.

She looked toward him, waiting.

He reached to the back of her neck, and then tucked the tag of her dress back down beneath her dress. "Perfect."

She blushed and reached behind her neck, to make sure her dress was now right. "Thank you."

"You're welcome," he said. "Ready?"

"Ready."

He placed his hand on the small of her back and walked with her to his truck. There, he opened the door for her.

As she climbed into his truck, he said, "I'm taking you to Coronado Beach after dinner. You can walk on the same beach Marilyn Monroe walked on, when filming *Some Like it Hot*."

"Isn't that also where the Navy SEALs train?"

"Yes. It's one of the places they train," he said.

He closed her door and went around to the driver's side and got in. Starting the truck up, he said, "Hungry?"

"Yes," she said. "A little bit."

. . .

CECELIA'S STOMACH was full of butterflies. This was their first official date. She wasn't sure she'd be able to eat.

But this is Brian.

It wasn't like she didn't know him. She tried to ignore the butterflies and just enjoy his company as she always had.

There's so much pressure on a first date. And on a first kiss. That's enough to make anyone nervous.

"I'm taking you to Tom Ham's Lighthouse Restaurant," he said. "It's right on the water, and there's an actual functioning lighthouse, known as Beacon Number Nice, on the U.S Coast Guard maps that they incorporated into the design. So, it's a well-known landmark in San Diego."

"Oh, wow," she said. "That sounds very cool."

There wasn't a hint in her expression or her voice that she wished she could see the landmark and the ocean. Only an excitement to go and experience it.

He'd purposefully chosen a place that would be near the water, so she could hear it and smell the scents of the ocean.

They were seated outside, as close to the water

as they could get, after he pressed a twenty into the palm of the person in charge of seating arrangements, saying, "I want to be as near the ocean as we can be," and then gesturing to Cecelia so the man would understand he was doing this for her.

He'd put a lot of thought into where he might take her. Candlelight or decorations on the walls weren't what he was looking for, but this was. She might hear the water lapping or the gulls cawing.

It seemed he'd chosen well, because every so often, she would pause and be still, listening, and then she would smile and carry on.

There was immense pleasure in seeing how much she was enjoying herself, at happiness glowing on her face.

She enjoyed her Caesar salad and a bite of his lobster bisque soup, which he delivered to her on his spoon, being careful not to spill it. Both their movements were slow, cautious, much like their date. It seemed the ease of their companionship had changed once what they were on an official date. Everything moved slowly, like the waves lapping upon the shore and the boats shifting against the docks as the sun went down.

They were both very quiet.

"Good?" he asked her to break the quiet.

"Very good," she said.

"If you'd like more, I'd be happy to share," he said. "Or we could order you a cup or a bowl."

"No, no," she said, shaking her head. "I'm not eating soup in a nice restaurant. It's too easy to drip."

"It's okay, Cecelia," he said. "No one's looking. There's just us and the water to the side here. No one is watching you."

"No, I'm fine," she said, sticking her fork into another piece of romaine. "I am enjoying the salad."

She'd ordered seared scallops, and he wondered if that would be enough. Maybe he could convince her to have dessert. And maybe she would try some of his paella, which came with saffron rice, fish, shrimp, chicken, chorizo, mussels, clams, peas and peppers. Much more than he would be able to eat.

And he had enjoyed feeding her the soup. He would happily feed her anything she wanted.

"Do you know that your smile can light up the whole room?" he asked.

"No," She blushed.

"You bring so much joy to everyone around you," he said.

"I, thank you," she said, seeming embarrassed by the turn in conversation."

"And here is our main course," he said.

"They smell delicious," she said.

The food was delicious, and she did try several bites of the different things in his paella.

Later when they were done, she turned down dessert.

"We can always get an ice cream, after we walk on the beach, if your sweet tooth kicks in," he said.

"Okay," she said. "I'm so full now though, I have no desire for a sweet."

The waiter brought the check, and Brian paid for their meal, leaving a good tip.

"Ready to go?" he asked. "Or would you like to enjoy this for a bit longer." He could always add on a coffee if she wanted to linger.

"I'm ready," she said. "The air is cooler now that the sun is down. I think it might be chilly later."

"True." He stood, pushing his chair back, and moved around to her chair.

She rose, accepted his arm, and as they were walking toward the entrance she leaned in and said, "I need to find a ladies room."

"Yes," he said. "I'll take you there and wait outside."

"Thank you," she said.

"Of course," he said.

He took her to the door of the ladies' room and said, "Straight ahead."

She pulled her collapsible cane out of her bag, and after putting it together, used it as she moved forward and pushed on the door.

This had been their routine many times on the trip out to San Diego, and he was quite used to it by now.

If they were going to be together long term, and he had the feeling that they were, this would become a pattern neither of them even thought about in the future.

Like watching his grandfather with his grandmother.

There had been something so loving about the way they'd looked after each other. He'd known since he was a young boy that, if he ever married, he wanted the relationship to be just like theirs.

Those manners though, they seemed to be from another time.

He wondered what his grandparents would have said about that, and what they would have thought of Cecelia. He was almost certain they both would have approved of his new girlfriend.

Tonight, he would kiss her. Normally he wouldn't have told her ahead of time, but he just couldn't see how to handle a first kiss any other way when the woman was blind.

What if she doesn't see it coming and it startles her, taking her too much by surprise?

He wasn't going to risk that. He didn't want anything to go wrong. With Cecelia, he would ask before he made any moves, and he would wait for each yes from her.

When she came out from the ladies' room, she put her cane away again and took hold of his arm. Then she smiled up at him. "Ready," she said.

He walked her to the truck and helped her in. "Ready to walk on the beach?" he asked.

"Yes," she said. "Let's leave our shoes. I like to feel the sand beneath my feet."

"Okay," he said. "There's a spot near the entrance where we can leave them. Then we won't have to carry them."

"Good," she said.

He drove them to the parking area that they would have to walk from, and then he got out, came around to open her door, and helped her down again.

He threaded his hand through hers and began

to walk slowly with her, toward the beach.

Once they reach the entrance, he picked a place for them to leave their shoes. They took off their shoes and left them.

He would hold her hand and he would help her if she had trouble on the sand or in the water.

They walked toward the water's edge, where the sand was wet and cooler. Now that the sun was down, the sand and the water would cool more and more, releasing the warmth the sun had put there all day.

She stopped and wiggled her toes into the wet sand, and then giggled. When she repeated the movements, her giggle became bigger.

"Does it tickle?" he asked, his feet getting wet and somewhat chilled.

"Yes, and it's cold, but I love it," she said, her voice breathy and full of joy. "I haven't done this in forever."

"I'm glad you're enjoying it," he said and smiled.

"When I lived in Atlantic Beach, North Carolina, that's where the Rosewood Center is, I was newly blind." She grew serious. "I was afraid of everything. Noises in the house at night, bumping into things or falling down the stairs, going out on the deck, falling down on the dunes. But mostly I was afraid of walking toward the ocean. And of touching it."

"I can understand that," he said.

"I felt like the waves would come in and pull me right back out, and I would fall down under the water and never come up again. And because the ocean is so big and powerful and can do that, I wouldn't walk near it for the longest time.

But then one day, I did, with the help of all my sisters there. Two held my hands, and one held onto me from behind, and I could hear the others. None of them were going to let the ocean take me. So, I went with them and I stood, just like this, and let the water touch my toes and come in and go out again, and I was reborn, like a child who had just learned to love a new thing. They gave the ocean and the beach back to me, those sisters. And I will love them forever for it."

He had tears in his eyes, hearing her story, and he squeezed her hand but didn't speak.

"It's good that you're holding my hand," she said. "But I think you can let go this time."

"Okay," he said, and he let go.

She stretched out her fingers, and then pulled them back in and took one step forward. The water rolled in and rolled out. Then did it again.

He watched her face for any sign of fear, but what he saw instead was courage, and a large smile starting to spread across her face. He didn't need her to tell him that she was conquering more of her fears.

And he was so very proud of her.

After a few more moments she turned to him and held out her hand. "Let's walk."

He took her hand and pulled her close. With his other hand, he brushed the hair from her face then cupped her cheek.

Her smile deepened.

He ran his thumb across her lips, brushing them. A light stroke.

Her lips parted.

He leaned in, sure of the moment, and brushed her lips with his. Not yet a kiss, but a light brushing, tentative yet sure.

CECELIA REVELED in all the sensations she felt. The sand beneath her, the water around her feet. The ocean breezes. The touch of his hand, holding hers.

Then he stopped on the sand and pulled her close to kiss her. First, his thumb brushing her lips and making them tingle, bringing all her senses more alive. Then his lips brushing hers, ever so gently.

His breath carried whispers of the warm minty scent of the breath mint he'd had earlier, after they'd eaten.

She wanted to taste him. Her lips opened, just enough to invite him in.

His lips brushing hers, increased pressure, and the tip of his tongue touched her lips, tickling, teasing, and then easing inside to touch the tip of her tongue.

Her breath hitched as she was caught up in new sensations and the feel and taste of his tongue.

Her hands moved up his shoulders and around to the back of his neck, holding on to him as his kiss threatened to sweep her away into overwhelming sensations, much like the ocean would have swept her away had she waded deep enough.

She waded deeper into their kiss.

It was a kiss as deep and sweeping as the sea, as soft and loving as the breeze, and as steady as the rocks along the shore. More memorable than anything either of them had done before.

For it was a soulmate's kiss, and down deep in their souls, they knew this was a true love's kiss.

CHAPTER 6

THE NEXT DAY, when Brian picked up Cecelia to take her to the hospital, he realized she had a glow she hadn't carried before.

It was a glow of deep happiness, and he was pretty sure he knew what had put it there.

"Did you sleep well?" he asked, hoping for a positive answer, and he was pleased when she smiled.

"Yes, I slept all night and didn't have one nightmare. I had a very nice dream instead."

"You did?"

"Mm-hmm."

"Going to tell me about it?"

"No, not this time," she said, with a blush and a smile.

Oh ho, one of those kinds of dreams, he thought, and smiled to himself. *I can just imagine.* "That's okay. You don't need to tell me. I'm glad you had a good one and hope that continues."

"Me, too," she said.

They picked up breakfast at a drive through, then drove on to the hospital, as he needed to drop her there and then go to his appointment.

He rode up the elevator to Sam's hospital room with her, saw that she was settled in a chair to visit, and then after telling them both goodbye, he hurried to his truck.

The sooner he took care of all his business, the sooner he could get back to his new girlfriend. He couldn't wait to spend more time with her and was going to ask her where she would like to go for dinner tonight.

WHILE CECELIA WAS VISITING SAM, and Brian had gone back to the base for his appointment, the fire alarm went off in the hallway outside Sam's hospital room.

Cecelia jumped. "What's that?" she said. "Is there a fire? What's going on?"

"The fire alarms are going off," Sam said. "I can see one flashing. But I don't see any smoke or fire. I'll call the nurse."

Someone entered the room and a man's voice said, "No, don't call. Everyone will be calling the nurses' station. They're busy. The nurses can't be everywhere."

His hand closed over Cecelia's arm. "Come with me," he said in a calm voice.

"Who are you?" she asked, her voice rising in fear.

"I'm a doctor," he said.

"It's okay," Sam said. "He's a doctor. Go with him."

"What about you?" Cecelia asked, looking toward Sam. She put her hand on the doctor's arm. "We need to get her out of here!"

The man put pressure on her arm, urging her away, toward the door. "The orderly is coming with a gurney to get your friend, and he'll take her out. Come with me. We have to take the stairs, and I'll help you down them."

She let the doctor guide her into the hall, where people were hurrying, and voices were coming from all over the floor. It sounded like pandemonium, and she couldn't see people or tell which way he was leading her, as they dodged in and out between people who were hurrying to get out.

They moved down the hall and to a stairwell where he held open the door with one hand and pulled her with the other, saying, "Come on."

Someone came up behind them. "Don't block the door," the woman said. "Let us out."

"I don't have my cane," Cecelia said, just as she realized she'd left her cane in the room.

"You don't need it," the doctor said. "I'm going to help you down the stairs." He pulled her through the doorway. "Come on, we need to keep moving and not block these people. Hold on to the railing."

She put her hand on the railing, and started carefully stepping down each step, with him holding onto her other arm, urging her down the stairs.

He spoke encouraging words to her, as she found each step with her foot, but it felt like it was taking forever, and they had four flights to go down.

She felt bad about being so slow and holding people up who wanted out so badly.

Many other people were taking the stairs, which got more and more crowded as they descended. Some people pushed past them, and others were more polite. Everyone was in a hurry to get out of the building.

She worried about Sam and hoped the person with the gurney had already taken her out.

Finally, they were on the bottom floor, and he helped her through the lobby and outside.

The breeze on her face was a relief, and she took a deep breath of fresh air.

She hadn't smelled any smoke on the way down, so that was good. She hoped they got all the patients out and wondered where they'd be taking Sam.

The doctor who'd helped her was still there, and he said, "Here, they're starting to move the gurneys out and need room." He pulled on her arm again. "We have to move out of the way."

Listening to him and letting him move her away from where people milled about, she went with him to a quieter area.

He said, "I see an empty bench over there. Come on, I'll get you seated, and then you'll have to wait while I go help get the others out."

She moved where he wanted her to, and then he let go of her and stepped away.

Cecelia turned her head right and then left, listening. The only thing she heard was traffic.

Where am I? Where did he go? And where was that bench he was talking about?

She reached out her hands and found only air.

Now what?

She needed her cane. And it was too quiet here. There were no people that she could hear. There was only traffic.

"Hello?" she called, not even knowing the doctor's name.

In their hurry to get out of the building, she hadn't thought to ask.

No one answered, but a vehicle pulled up near her. She reached out with her foot, trying to feel where the curb was, as the vehicle sounded close.

Someone stepped behind her.

Suddenly, a man's hand was on her mouth, holding duct tape, sticky and thick.

No!

Another man wrapped his arms around hers, holding her so she couldn't move.

The duct tape was slapped down over her mouth by the first man, and pressed hard onto her lips, to keep her mouth closed.

She could still breathe through her nose, but now she started to hyperventilate, fast.

What's happening? Who was that man who helped me out of the hospital? Where did he go? Who are these men?

She heard a van door slide open.

What can I do?

She tried to turn right and left to get free, but the man holding her arms was too strong. Hands grabbed her, pulling her into the van.

She kicked her legs, trying to fight, but her legs were then grabbed by strong hands, and she was manhandled all the way into the van.

The van door slid closed, slamming as her heart beat fast in her chest. Ropes were tied around her wrists and ankles. She tried to fight, but they were too strong.

Where are they taking me? What do they want with me? How will Brian find me?

She hadn't had time to press the pendant to alert Brian that she needed him. And she needed him more than ever, now.

Cecelia brought her bound wrists up, curling into herself, and they didn't stop her. Pressing against her chest, where the pendant lay between her breasts, she hoped she'd activated the pendant tracking device.

Her arms were grabbed and forced down again as they held her down.

The pinprick of a needle going into her arm made her breathe in sharply.

Then everything in her world went black.

BRIAN WASN'T BACK from his appointment at the Naval base, when the tracking device on his phone went off.

Cecelia needed him.

He needed to get back.

Brian hurried to his truck and headed for the hospital.

When he stepped into the hospital elevator and pressed the elevator buttons, the braille panels reminded him of Cecelia.

In the elevator, riding up, one of the female passengers said, "I'm glad there wasn't really a fire. Can you imagine trying to move all these patients?"

Her girlfriend said, "I know. How would they get them all out fast enough?"

He went on alert the moment the first woman said "fire." He looked at them and said, "There was a fire alarm?"

"Yes. You must've missed it," the first woman said. "This was a couple of hours ago."

He took out his cell phone and double checked it.

No messages.

Cecelia hadn't messaged. He'd heard nothing from about a fire. And she was afraid of fires. Had nightmares about them. It didn't seem like her not to call or text him, to tell him about the fire alarms going off.

Something was wrong.

He had a bad feeling about this. A gut feeling.

Had she left the hospital when the fire alarm went off on her own? Or had she gone with someone else?

His gut was telling him she'd been taken. But he had to double check with her cousin.

The two women got off on the third floor as he impatiently waited for the fourth floor.

He needed to see Cecelia now and to know she was okay.

The doors opened, and he hurried to Sam's room.

Cecelia wasn't in the room. But her cane was leaning against the wall. He frowned when he saw it.

Sam was looking at him quizzically.

They both spoke at once. "Where's Cecelia?"

"She's not with you?" Sam asked, her face showing concern.

"No," he said. "Tell me what happened."

"There was a fire alarm, and people started going outside," she said. "She left with one of the doctors."

"What did he look like?" Brian pulled out his phone to check the tracking device.

The tracking device was still working. Still turned on.

She'd been taken and there was no point in searching the hospital.

The device showed she was already gone from the building.

"She's not here and my app notified me she wasn't here, soon after she was away from the hospital," he said then glanced at Sam.

"Oh no," Sam said. "What's happened to her?"

"I can track her and I'm going to find her." Without another word, he was out the door, intent on following the GPS as it showed movement.

At the elevator, he punched the button and impatiently waited for the doors to open.

When they opened, he stepped in, and once the doors opened on the ground floor, he left at a run.

Getting in his truck, he started in the direction she'd gone, following that path.

They had headed for Mexico. The Mexican border was only thirty minutes from the hospital.

They'd moved her over the border. She was in Mexico.

Fast and easy to get in, she'd now be in Mexico with only her driver's license. If she still had her driver's license on her. They might have taken it away.

Did she even own a passport? Had she ever left the country? Did she want to travel outside the United States?

So many questions he hadn't been able to ask her yet. They were still getting to know each other.

He doubted she had traveled much, if at all.

She'd never left Three C's Ranch since she'd started working there to go anywhere other than an appointment in town.

She'll be terrified right now, and have no idea where she was being taken, or for what reason.

Mexico was close. So quick and easy to take her over the border.

Damn it.

A pretty silver haired woman who was blind was a soft target.

She'd caught the eye of someone who wanted her, and they'd taken her. This kind of thing happened every day. More than people realized. But not to his girl.

They'd taken the wrong woman.

He would make every one of these assholes wish they'd never laid eyes on her.

But first, he had to find her.

Was Mexico even their final destination?

I need to find her fast and get her out.

CHAPTER 7

CECELIA STOOD, somewhat groggily, from whatever they'd injected her with to knock her out. She had no idea where she was but sensed no one was with her.

It was too quiet. So quiet she could hear her own breathing.

She moved forward, her hands held out in front of her to touch and feel what was around her. She found the rusty metal door they'd brought her through.

She remembered the clang of the metal door closing and the sound of a lock after they'd thrown her into the room, dazed and just waking up for the shot. Too dizzy and disoriented to even stand up by herself.

Now, she could stand and walk but was still woozy.

She felt her way around, looking for something, anything that would help her get out. Her fingers moved from the metal door to the wall on the right and across the wall, helping her to "look."

The wall felt bumpy, sandpapery, like rough concrete beneath her fingers. It was like touching a driveway, which made her situation even more surreal to her, this rough surface being the material of the wall, not a floor or driveway.

Where am I? Still in San Diego?

No.

There were voices. Speaking Spanish. Was she in Mexico? Mexico wasn't that far.

Oh God. I'm in Mexico. They've taken me out of the country.

Her stomach dropped, and she nearly gagged at the stink of the room when she turned to the next wall and the strong smell of urine wafted up from the ground there. A fly buzzed near her ear, and she waved at it, shooing it away.

She wished she could see her feet, to know if she might be stepping in something. But maybe it was better she couldn't see when the stench was so bad—here, where people had obviously relieved themselves. At least, she was still wearing her tennis shoes and not sandals.

Mexico. I'm in Mexico. He'll never find me here.

Her heart sank.

She found no window on the first wall with the door and none on the second to the right. Now, she moved along the third wall and felt a slight breeze, quickly gone, as if it had never been there.

Sounds came from up high. A window. She reached her hands up, as high as she could reach.

The window was too high for her to reach touch even a sill, if it had one.

The room was hot.

Her jeans were sticking to her as if they'd been painted on, and her T-shirt was wet with sweat. Another drop of sweat rolled down her back, beneath the waistband of her jeans.

How thirsty she was.

This room is not just hot, it is sweltering, and the drug they gave me is wearing off.

All her senses were fully waking up. Maybe that was not such a good thing in circumstances like these.

She found nothing on the fourth wall, and now she was back to the wall with the door.

This small room, no more than eight foot by

ten foot was now her prison, with one door and a window that did barely anything to help with the heat.

Is there water? I need water.

She realized she was dehydrated.

Next, she dropped down onto her hands and knees to search the floor, in case there was water there, somewhere.

Even a dog would be given a water bowl.

A dirt floor. Where the hell am I? Mexico somewhere, but where? How will anyone find me here?

The floor was dirt; there was no water. There was nothing else in the room, except a mattress on the floor. A stinky mattress she moved away from, into the center of the room.

She wrapped her arms around her knees, squatting on the ground, and began to cry.

I am in hell. The heat, the stink. I am in hell, and there are bad men here who are going to harm me. Maybe soon. Please God, get me out of here somehow. Please send Brian for me.

Then it came to her.

The pendant.

In her groggy, drugged state she had forgotten about the pendant. She'd pressed it once before they'd injected her.

Brian had made a plan if something were to happen to her. He'd prepared for this, and she'd forgotten.

Now that she remembered, she started pressing it frantically, over and over, praying that it still worked, crying as tears began to stream down her face.

BRIAN WAS DRIVING and following the GPS movements on his phone while trying not to get pulled over for speeding. The clock was ticking, and there was no way in hell he was following the speed limit.

I have to get to Cecelia before something even worse than being kidnapped happens.

Using the app on his phone to track her, via the pendant on her necklace, he knew she was across the border in Mexico.

The longer she wore the necklace undetected, the better. However, there was a very real possibility that her captors would find the pendant and remove it from her.

Following the route they'd taken, he drove toward the border.

He looked at his phone again. Movement on the GPS screen had stopped.

This could mean she was in a final location. Or in a final location, for now.

Ensenada.

That's where she is now.

He took his phone and dialed Arturo, a Mexican national who had dual citizenship. Brian and Arturo had served in the Marines together overseas, and then Arturo had decided not to re-enlist, but to return home to fight corruption in the city of his grandparents and his cousins. He was now a Mexican policeman, who trained the SWAT team.

Arturo answered, "*Hola.*"

"*Hola.* Arturo, this is Barbie," Brian said. Using that nickname, Arturo would know this was a serious call.

Instead of using Brian's "Barbie" nickname, Arturo called Brian his "brother from another mother", and the two of them had been as close as brothers. Only fellow Marines called Brian Barbie, a nickname he'd picked up in boot camp because his last name was Ken, and his sergeant had thought that was funny.

"*Amigo*, what are you up to?" The pleasure of hearing from his friend was in Arturo's voice.

"I'm in San Diego, getting ready to cross the border," Brian said. "Heading your way, and I need some help."

"Anything, *amigo*, I owe you at least one life," Arturo said.

"I came to San Diego with a woman who has been taken to Ensenada," Brian said. "I have the location, and I'm heading there *now*!"

"I am sorry to hear this. Tell me more," Arturo said, his tone now serious.

"I gave Cecelia a pendant necklace with a GPS device. After they took her, the GPS moved in a straight path to Ensenada," Brian said. "They've stopped. I need to get there fast and find her. The clock is ticking."

"Okay, *amigo*," Arturo said. "I will pick you up in Puerto Nuevo about halfway there, and we can travel together. Then I will help you find your woman."

"Thank you, brother," Brian said, with a catch in his voice. Arturo would help him and would have his back.

When he reached the border, there was a line to cross over into Mexico. A long line of cars.

Of course, there was. I should have thought of that.

This was not what he needed right now.

He cursed, wishing he'd had time to get to a helicopter, so he could get up into the air to parachute in fast.

This way, he wouldn't be able to take his weapons in.

Dammit.

He should have thought of that, too. He shook his head to clear it. Worry over Cecelia reached into his emotions, and talking to Arturo had, too. He was too close to this operation, and he knew it.

Time to get his head on straight.

Do the job. Save the girl. Like any other girl.

He told himself that and forced his emotions back down where he wouldn't think about them again, until she was safe. There was no room for error here. He'd raced off, emotionally reacted, and that was not good.

He needed a plan.

He'd have to park the truck and walk across. That would be faster. Many Mexicans had cars on each side of the border for this very reason. It took too long waiting in the driving lines, and walking was faster and easier. His analytical brain had kicked in now, and he was thinking fast.

Rethinking his plan, he found a long-term parking lot and parked his truck. He placed his weapons in the glove box and left his backpack under the seat. Nothing to check meant a faster crossing over the border. A bag could slow him down. And he, himself, was a weapon. Other weapons he could pick up. He got out and locked his truck, stuck the keys in his pocket and started walking.

He picked up his phone and called again as he walked toward the border.

Arturo picked up on the first ring. "Brother, talk to me."

"The lines were too long," Brian said. "I left my truck in long term parking to walk across. I had to leave my weapons behind in my truck."

"I got you covered," Arturo said. "I'm already on the way to our meeting place."

Arturo would know exactly what weapons Brian needed and which he wanted. He would also know the area and where Cecelia might be held.

"I will meet you halfway as planned," Arturo said. "Can you take a taxi now?"

"Yes," Brian said. "Once I get through to Mexico."

"You will not have a problem," Arturo said. "But

if you do, you call me. When you get here, I will buy you a taco."

They'd had a standing agreement that when Brian made it to Mexico and looked Arturo up, Arturo would buy him a fish taco and bring a bottle of good tequila.

"Thank you, my brother," Brian said. "I may need that tequila when this is over."

"I will help you find your girl," Arturo said. "We will go in and get her together."

"Thank you, brother," Brian said.

"*De nada*," Arturo replied.

They both hung up.

The GPS showed no further movement. That could be good. Or bad.

He needed to get there in time, before they did anything worse to Cecelia than they already had.

At the border, he finally reached the check point. There was a line, but at least it was moving faster than the car line, since it was quicker patting a person down than it was looking through a vehicle.

They patted him down, looked at his passport, which he always carried, noted he was a U.S. Marine, and commented on it, and as he was carrying no drugs or weapons, they let him through.

After he was on the other side, he walked to where taxis waited.

He raised his hand and hollered, "Taxi!"

Eager drivers jockeyed for position to get his business, and soon, he was headed down the highway to his meeting with Arturo.

CECELIA SAT on the dirt floor in the middle of the room, her arms locked around her bent knees as she rocked and cried. The scents surrounding her were too much. Her nose was sensitive to scent, had been ever since she'd lost her sight and had to rely more upon it. Most of the time, having a heightened sense of smell was a good thing, but here, it was not. The stuff they'd injected into her had completely worn off, so now, she was fully aware of her environment.

No way was she sitting on that nasty mattress, which stunk to high heaven.

God only knows what has happened in this room.

She didn't even want to think about that, so she pushed the thought away. But from the stink coming off that mattress, she could well imagine. She wasn't going to touch it for any reason, unless she had to.

Her thumb found the pendant beneath her T-shirt again and she pressed it, hard, as if pressing harder would bring Brian faster.

Please find me. Please, please find me.

She repeated the mantra like a prayer and tried not to think about the possibility that she was too far out of range, where Brian couldn't find her.

She'd just have to keep pressing it and praying, while hoping those men didn't find the necklace and take it from her. There was nothing else she could do but pray and wait.

CHAPTER 8

Arturo was waiting for Brian with weapons, a bullet proof vest, a shield and helmet...and a fish taco.

Brian would have laughed had he not been so worried about Cecelia. The sight of Arturo with his trunk open, his SWAT weapons displayed, and holding a taco, was kind of funny.

"Brother," Arturo said, "welcome to Mexico." He handed him the taco and patted him on the back with the other arm. "You are looking good, *amigo*, but eat and keep up your strength."

Before he took a bite of the taco, Brian said, "Is this taco hot, or not hot, my spicy ninja brother?"

Brian had often called Arturo his "spicy ninja brother", and one of the Marines in their unit had even drawn a cartoon of him and labeled it, "The Spicy Ninja."

"Try this. It is not hot," was Arturo's phrase which had tripped up many men until they'd wised up.

"Not hot" had become code between these two brothers in arms, and it meant the situation might be FUBAR, but Arturo still believed you could handle it.

So now, though it had been several years since the two men had fought together, it all came back as naturally as if they'd been born to it and never left the life. For Brian, that felt really good.

If it wasn't for the fact that Brian's girl was in danger, they both would've smiled at being back, brothers reunited, fighting together. Instead, both men were focused on rescuing Cecelia.

"It is not hot," Arturo said. "You eat while I show you what I brought you. Then suit up and show me your GPS."

Arturo had fitted him out.

He had a Ka-Bar knife down his back, like old times, with a 9mm handgun on his right hip, and another pistol strapped to his ankle. With the AR in his hands and extra ammo hanging crisscrossed over his chest, he looked like freaking Rambo.

Brian couldn't have asked for more. Arturo had treated him as a brother would.

Add in the martial arts fighting skills Brian Meng Ken had grown up with, and the various styles he'd picked up in more recent years, the question was never which weapon he should use, but which of these fighting tools he would choose to use to win a battle.

He was a man who didn't deliberate long, but who knew almost in an instant, which tool was best, and unerringly selected the correct one. As a result, he rarely lost a fight.

Had there been tapes, his fighting style would have been analyzed as similar to Bruce Lee's, though he knew several other styles. Bruce had been the hero of Brian's childhood that he'd most wanted to emulate.

Martial arts had gone a long way to making him strong in mind, body, and spirit when he was a child and neighborhood boys had picked on him for being half "chink." In the martial arts community, his heritage was something to be proud of, and his father and grandfather were Chinese men he also looked up to. The Marines had simply added to his arsenal.

All this, Arturo, of course, knew, as the two of

them had fought often together, to the point where each knew what the other would do without the fancy high-tech equipment which allowed communication on an operation.

But given all that, it still felt good to be fitted out with the tools of his trade again, and to be going into the fight with his brother at his side.

The GPS device showed Brian and Arturo an area Arturo knew.

"There is an old abandoned warehouse there," he said. "The company went out of business. I don't know who owns it now."

Brian got into Arturo's car for the drive to Ensenada, thirty minutes away, and they headed down the highway.

GPS had still not moved, which meant they should catch up to them soon. They spent the drive catching up with each other. Arturo talked about his wife and kids, his old grandmother who was now one-hundred-and-three, and his American cousin who had joined the Marines last year.

When they arrived in the area, Arturo drove slowly past the warehouse once, and then circled back and came in from the other side. He'd spotted a place to park near an old building where it would be less noticeable. They would be moving in heavily armed, but he didn't want his car stolen or the tires removed.

The warehouse was in front of them, and they moved in closer. The GPS showed she was in a brown adobe building behind the old warehouse.

"Even if this warehouse is empty," Arturo said. "There may be squatters inside."

"Great," Brian said.

They would have to check out the larger building before checking out the smaller one, because the larger one would be at their backs when they entered the smaller hut, and they didn't want anyone sneaking up behind them.

The adobe building Cecelia was inside, looked like a small but long house, with a window the size of shoe box set ten-feet-high, near the tin roof, to allow for air flow in the heat. The open windows had no glass, and no screens, which also meant no air conditioning.

Brian could hardly stand the thought of her being in there and couldn't wait to get her out.

As he watched the building, his thoughts turned to what she might be going through.

Cecelia was in that building, and she'd be sweltering in this heat, likely getting more dehydrated by the minute.

After we get her out, I'll need to get water into her soon.

Already, he was thinking of the aftercare she might need. He had his medical kit in the toolbox of his truck and had been prepared for anything, but the truck was on the other side of the border, and he might have to get what she needed faster than he could get to what was in the truck.

Arturo might have to come through for him again, if she needed anything right away.

The warehouse was empty of people, but there were boxes stacked inside. Someone was using it for storing and shipping. There was a forklift in the middle of the building, and a folding table and one chair, which looked like a makeshift office for deals. A notepad and pen sat on the table. Arturo looked at the notepad, but it didn't say anything and provided no clue as to who was using the warehouse.

Since no one else was inside, they used the building to get closer to the adobe building, and watched it, to see how many men they would be dealing with.

Brian counted two men inside the adobe building, who had gone inside carrying cardboard boxes of supplies, and two men outside, one casually leaning on an old Jeep, while the other sat on a chair near the door, cleaning his fingernails with a large knife.

That made four men, that he knew of, armed with guns and knives. There might be more.

Brian didn't want to wait. He wanted to charge in.

Arturo whispered, "Wait until they finish carrying their stuff into the building, so they are all in one place and not moving around so much."

"You know the minute they're done; they're going to turn their attention to her," Brian said.

He wouldn't say it, but they both knew one of the first things those men were going to do was rape their captive.

And he didn't want them turning their attention to Cecelia. He wasn't waiting for shit. "I'm going in."

"Right behind you, brother," Arturo said. "You lead."

Brian moved toward the building on stealthy feet.

CHAPTER 9

THERE WAS one way into the building, and that was through the front door. Brian snuck to the wall next to that door and prepared to turn and shoot in through the doorway.

Now, he could see five men were in the front room, sitting around a table. Beer bottles sat on the table and on the floor next to their chairs. After carrying all those boxes in, they'd sat down to have a beer. Weapons were on the floor next to the men, and one long gun leaned against the wall.

The men who would shoot at Brian wouldn't know he was wearing a bullet proof Kevlar vest, he and wasn't stopping.

He would die before he'd lose Cecelia to them. But he didn't plan on losing.

He was there to win.

And then he was taking Cecelia home.

They had his girl. They were going down. Brian charged into the room, shooting.

Brian fired a double tap at the first man who reached for a weapon, and the man fell back, the first shot in the chest, a kill shot, the second that followed, simply habit.

A man to his right rushed him with a knife, but Brian moved forward and to the man's right flank, grabbing his wrist in a quick move, and twisting the knife away from himself, he turned it on his attacker.

Arturo had followed him and double tapped, shooting the third man, who hit the wall with a smear of blood before sliding toward the floor.

A fourth man ran down the hallway toward a room with a closed door and was trying to unlock that door.

The fifth man's gun jammed when he tried to shoot, and he was reaching for another gun when Brian shot him with the double tap Marines trained to do.

Knifed guy was moaning and reaching for a gun on the floor, but Arturo tapped him twice when he shot.

They were all dead except the guy down the hall, who had disappeared into that room.

Brian ran down the hall and pushed open the door.

The fourth man stood in the middle of a small room, holding Cecelia in front of him. He had a gun pointed at Cecelia's head.

She stood frozen, her gaze looking toward the ceiling, and her lips trembling. Tears rolled from her eyes.

Then her gaze dropped and looked toward him.

"Brian," she gasped out.

"I'm here," he said, to reassure her that he was. "And I'm taking you out of here."

"One step," the fifth man said. "One step toward me, and I blow her brains out."

"Let her go," Brian said.

"Back away, out of this room," the man said, his lips curling into a sneer. "I am walking out of here with her, but you have to move out of the way, first."

Brian backed up, and then stepped out of the room, still standing in the doorway, facing the man and Cecelia.

Arturo's head now appeared in a window along the back wall of the room. How he'd gotten up there, Brian didn't know. But he was there, and so was the gun he aimed at the fifth gunman, waiting for a good shot. An expert marksman, he would take the shot if he had an opening.

Brian needed to keep the gunman in the room. If he allowed the man to leave, the shot would be lost.

"No, I don't think so," Brian said. "I can't let you leave with her."

"You have no other choice, *amigo*," the fifth man snarled. He moved forward, pushing Cecelia in front of him.

She stumbled on her untied shoelace, and her arms went out in front of her as if she would fall. Off balance, her head went down.

Arturo took the shot.

The fifth man dropped, a bullet to the back of his head, and he fell to the ground.

Cecelia was covered in a spray of blood, bone, and brains.

Brian went to her, one arm still holding his gun away from her as he wrapped his other arm around her, pulling her close.

"Brian, you came for me!" Cecelia cried out.

"I told you I would," he said, quietly, hoping to

calm her. "You're safe now. We're getting you out of here."

"I was so scared," she said. "I was afraid the GPS wouldn't work from so far away, and that you'd never find me again."

"Not a chance," he said. "I would've found a way to locate you, no matter where you were, and I will always come for you." He slung the gun over his shoulder.

She was crying and hanging onto him now.

He bent and lifted her up into his arms to carry her outside to Arturo's car. "I've got you now, babe," he said. "You're safe, and we're going home. Back to the United States of America, and I'm not leaving your side until you're safe back at the ranch. Sound okay to you?"

"More than okay. I want to go home," she said. "With you. Take me home, Brian."

"Good, I was hoping you'd say that. I was afraid I would lose you," he said, finally admitting it out loud, now that they were outside. "I was afraid I would never get to kiss you again." He set her down on the ground so she could stand again.

"I was afraid you'd never find me," she said. "I thought, if I died down here, at least you had kissed me one night, on the beach, beneath the stars. I would always know that kiss, what it felt like kissing you. I would always remember our first and only kiss."

"Not the only one," he said as he took out a handkerchief and wiped her face, clearing away the blood and sweat. "We can fix that right now." Placing both of his palms on her cheeks, he brought her face close to him then pressed his lips against hers in a fierce kiss.

She responded by kissing him back with just as much fervor.

Their kiss deepened as their tongues touched, teased, and danced. They kissed as if they couldn't get enough of each other. Passion, desire, longing, relief and happiness were all in the mix of this kiss, and it was another they would remember for a lifetime.

ACROSS THE BORDER, back in the U.S., Brian and Cecelia were sharing a room at the fanciest hotel in San Diego.

He'd ordered champagne and strawberries, and they'd made plans to not leave the room until the next day at eleven, when it was time to check out.

Life was short, and they'd both agreed that they wanted to make the most of it, here, tonight. Making love for the first time, together as a couple.

He wasn't letting Cecelia out of his sight for a long while. Nearly losing her had scared him and made him realize how much he cared for her.

They might even be picking out a ring soon, if things went as he hoped they would go.

The events in Mexico had changed them both.

Tonight, would be the beginning of a new future for them, and he couldn't wait.

THE END

MONTANA MARINE

Debra Parmley

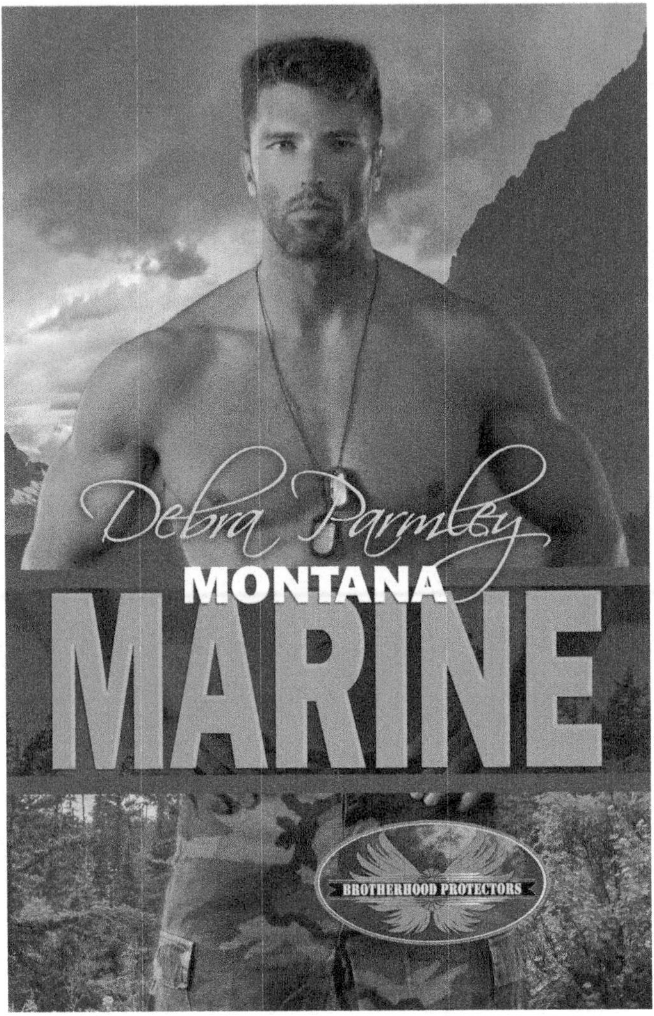
Debra Parmley
MONTANA
MARINE
BROTHERHOOD PROTECTORS

CHAPTER 1

GUNNERY SERGEANT JACK "GUNNY" Barr had been on edge all day, but couldn't put his finger on the cause. It had started in the morning when he'd walked outside and looked up at the sky as the sun rose. A peculiar red filled the sky, giving him a slight feeling of foreboding. Though not a single thing had fallen into place to confirm the feeling until now.

The Marine Second Force Recon team was in the area after completing another mission when a broadcast for help came over the clear channel of the radio, calling all United States units in the area. SEAL team ten was in trouble. The pilot circled the helicopter around and headed back to give them aid. Then it all went to hell.

AXEL SVENSON AKA "SWEDE" was the one person in the hospital Gunny spent the most time talking to. Marine Recon guys didn't usually mix with other Navy personnel, but Swede was a SEAL and they'd met during a mission that had gone bad. There was no one else in the hospital either of them could talk to about what had gone down that day. Partly because of the security clearance, and partly because only someone who'd been there would really understand. Swede had lost a team member and had a traumatic brain injury. Gunny was concerned about Swede because TBI's could be serious. By the time Gunny had been released to go home, they'd developed a friendship that began with bonding over the incident.

Gunny was now home and retired from the Marines all of three months, which was making him stir crazy. He'd been making repairs to the small house he owned after he'd finished making the rounds and visiting with all the family and friends that had wanted to see him after he got out. Now that he was back, it was time to work on the house. There was still a lot to be done. Amazing how that list added up after being away from the house for so many years on one deployment after another.

The phone rang, and when Gunny picked it up, he said, "Hello."

Swede was on the line.

"Hey Gunny, how you doing?"

"I'm doing great. What's up, shipmate? How've you been?"

"I'm out, Gunny. Got the doc's all clear."

"That's good news. Glad to hear it."

"I'm in Montana."

"Nice. Fishing?"

"No. Working. Got a proposition for you."

"All right. Let's hear it."

"A buddy of mine started a bodyguard service out here in Montana. The Brotherhood Protectors. We could use another good man. I thought of you. And the job pays well."

"What's the job? Who are you protecting?"

"Angelica Glory."

"No shit?" Gunny whistled.

"Monroe Witham, her manager, just hired us. She's got a stalker, Gunny."

"I'm on board. When and where? Give me the details. "

"Monroe says he'll fly her out of L.A., quick.

Said they'd be here in three days."

Gunny laughed. "Civilians don't know the meaning of quick."

Swede laughed.

They'd both been on many missions where they'd been roused from sleep and had to grab gear and be wheels up within minutes.

"No, they don't."

"You just tell me when and where you need me and I'm there."

Swede gave him the rest of the details, and then hung up. Gunny glanced around the room he'd been working on and then stood, leaving his tools where they lay. There was nothing here that couldn't wait until he got back. He'd pack and then head out for an early dinner and a beer.

At the bar, he texted his brother.

Got a new job. Headed to Montana.

THE NEXT NIGHT, unable to sleep, Gunny fired up his computer and started to search. His first assignment was for one of the sexiest women in

Hollywood. Angelica Glory. She'd stand out anywhere she went, and it appeared she loved to stand out.

A quick internet search told him Angelica loved to party in the clubs. Tabloid speculation about who her latest lover was seemed to change month to month. None of this was fact. He had her dossier in front of him, which listed everyone personally connected to her. It was quite detailed, but anything further he found would be added to it. The dossier listed everyone close to her. Family, close friends, and boyfriends. The names on the list were only a fraction of the names listed by the tabloids.

Angelica's pattern appeared to be relationships with well-known actors, which lasted anywhere from six months to two years. None of her relationships had hit the three-year mark.

A major storm had kept him grounded in Houston, Texas, and now Miss Glory and her assistant would be arriving in Montana the night before he did. But the rest of the team would be in place. He'd be working with Swede, who would also be their computer guru. Hank 'Montana' Patterson was the third man. Montana, who ran the Brotherhood Protectors, was no stranger to Gunny, as Montana and Swede had been on the same SEAL team that fateful day.

The three-man team would work sixteen hours on, eight off in staggered shifts, so there would always be two men on duty at any time. Gunny would be man on point, getting to know Angelica and Lucy and gathering intel to help the team do their jobs. Swede would handle the technical aspects of the job. Montana had other bodyguards working for him and other clients, so he'd have the satellite phone. Cell phone service was poor to non-existent at the house. They'd be using two-way radios, and all their equipment was encrypted to prevent the stalker from listening in.

Swede had dug up plenty of intel for the dossier, but Gunny liked to look at things himself and get a feel for the situation. He much preferred seeing imagery to words on paper.

There were plenty of images of Angelica Glory. Plenty of cleavage to look at, and she liked showing it off. Great body. Carried herself with class in some images and with a haughty air in others. She loved the camera. Pictures could tell you so much.

Lucy Woods, the assistant, now she was intriguing. Pretty woman with long, silky black hair, pale skin, and pretty blue eyes. He noted one mannerism she had of tilting her head to the right and looking up at the camera. Did she know she did that? She didn't like the camera much. He wondered if the movement developed from being a shy woman with a wish to hide.

He'd meet them soon enough. Closing the computer down, he went to bed and forced himself to go to sleep.

HIS BROTHER CALLED the next day as Jack was at the airport. Jack was glad his brother had security clearance, because then he could be truthful when talking about his new job. He and his twin had few secrets and shared an uncanny way of sensing when the other had something going on. Hank Patterson had not only okayed it, he'd asked if Jack's brother might be interested in a job.

"Hey, Ted."

"Jack, I got your message the other day. Been flying. What's up? You got a new job?"

"Yeah. Bodyguard."

"No shit. That's great. Thought you were retired, though."

"I'm too young to retire. Not used to all this sitting around. Nothing to do but fix this house."

"I hear ya. Can't imagine not flying. We're both too young to retire. So who are ya working for?"

"Brotherhood Protectors. It's a bodyguard service made up of SEALs and former combat vets started by Hank Patterson. His family has a ranch in Eagle Rock, Montana."

"Where's Eagle Rock? Never heard of it."

"I had to look it up too. It's in the foothills of the Crazy Mountains in the southwest corner of Montana. Hills and mountains to the west, plains to the east. Bear Creek Ranch is Patterson's ranch."

"Sounds interesting. Crazy Mountains, huh. Skiing?"

"Yeah, they've got skiing. Big Sky Resort. Biggest ski resort in Montana, and it's only forty miles south. There's also the Bridger Bowl Ski area near the Bridger Mountains."

"I'll come out and see ya this winter then. We'll hit the slopes."

"Sounds good. Yellowstone National Park isn't

far if you come out sooner. Temps are in the nineties right now. About the same as here."

"Montana is all cowboys and cattle ranches. Why would anyone need a bodyguard out there?"

"The rich and famous come out and buy cattle ranches, horse ranches. They want privacy and seclusion. This first assignment is for Miss Angelica Glory."

"The actress?"

"Yep."

"Damn, she's hot. That's a plum assignment."

"Maybe. We'll see. I'm at Sugarland right now getting ready to board in fifteen minutes."

"What are you flying out on?"

Jack grinned. Ted, a pilot in the Air Force, knew planes. He'd appreciate this one.

"A Lear thirty five."

"Nice jet."

"Sure beats flying commercial."

"Sure does. Okay. Give me a heads up when you get the new address."

"Will do."

~

IT BEGAN SO CASUALLY, no one suspected Miss Angelica Glory had a stalker. With so many fans from all around the world, she often received gifts, cards, and letters. So when a single red rose was delivered to Miss Glory's trailer on the set location in L.A. for the movie she was shooting, Lucy Wood, Angelica's assistant, put the rose in a vase with water and filed the silly note away in the filing cabinet with the fan mail. Angelica's fans sent her notes that said all sorts of things, some of them quite silly in Lucy's opinion.

This card said, one rose for all the ways I'm going to spoil you. – The man of your dreams.

From a regular boyfriend, it would have been a sweet note to receive, but Angelica was currently without a boyfriend and too busy wrapping up her latest movie to have time for one. Lucy shook her head at the note, but didn't think any more about it.

Every day following, for twenty-three more days, the red roses arrived and they came with the same note, typed in the old fashioned way, with a typewriter using black ink on white paper. By day twenty-four, Lucy Wood was fed up with red roses and silly notes from secret admirers, though she kept her feelings to herself.

Day twenty-five came and went with no deliveries and nothing to file away. On day twenty-seven, Lucy was in the bedroom of Angelica's trailer on the set, putting away clothes Angelica had strewn across the bed, when someone knocked on the trailer door.

"Coming," she called out and hurried to the door to open it. A deliveryman stood with a package instead of the usual florist delivery person. Taking the package from him, she saw Angelica hurrying across the lot, calling, "Is that for me?"

"Yes, it is," Lucy called back, noting there was no return address on the small, brown package. Angelica hurried up and took the package out of Lucy's hands. She went into her trailer and Lucy followed. Angelica sat on the couch and began opening the package as Lucy sat beside her.

Ripping and tearing, Angelica was like an impatient child at Christmas. Once the package was open, her eyes lit at the red, lacy thing inside. Red was her favorite color.

"What is it?" Lucy asked, leaning closer.

Angelica lifted it up, so Lucy could see it was a red lace, see-through baby doll nightie. A note fluttered down onto the ground.

Lucy picked the note up and handed it to Angelica.

The note read, Wear this tonight, the man of your dreams.

"What is this supposed to mean? Wear this tonight? I don't have a date tonight." Angelica crumpled the note and tossed it to the floor.

Lucy picked it up and placed it to the side. She'd file it later.

"No one gives me orders telling me what to wear." Angelica's tone became haughtier with each word. "The cup size is too small for me, it will never fit my boobs." Angelica thrust the nightie at Lucy, saying, "Here, you take it, it will fit yours."

While true, the way Angelica said it sounded insulting to Lucy, who was far from the double D's Angelica proudly showed off after her breast augmentation surgery. She liked showing off her cleavage and her bare breasts, and she liked the attention they brought her.

Though it wasn't a subject Lucy thought about much, the size of her breasts having never been much of a big deal before coming to work for Angelica, Lucy was no more than a C cup on a good day. Unfortunately, her boss had developed a nasty habit of finding ways to put Lucy down, and this was one of them.

Taking the lace nightie, Lucy looked at it. It would fit her. She'd tuck it away for a special night with a special guy, if she ever had one. Which did not seem likely as long as she was working for Angelica. But maybe one day. And if not, she'd use the lace to make something else. Folding the nightie up, she said, "Thank you," before tucking it into her big shoulder bag.

Angelica often handed off perfectly good things she was tired of, or new things she'd never worn. Luckily, Lucy's sewing skills enabled her to make all manner of things out of these cast offs and they, along with the jewelry she designed, sold at Bejeweled and Bedazzled, her online Etsy store. While she'd hoped to work in Hollywood as a costume designer one day, for now, she poured her creativity into making her jewelry while working for Miss Glory.

As Angelica left the trailer without acknowledging Lucy's thank you, Lucy picked up the note and frowned. This note was signed the same way as the notes that came with the roses. She'd check to be sure, but after seeing the same note so many days in a row, she was quite sure the same person sent it.

She went into the office that evening to check and see if she was right about the notes. She opened the filing cabinet and pulled them out and laid them all on the table. Now there was no question in her mind.

The notes were from the same person. The roses were nice, but now sending lingerie? And that note. I have a bad feeling about this. Maybe I should call Monroe.

If Angelica's secret admirer was someone who knew her at all, he'd have known not to speak to her the way he had in the note. It would not go over well. This had to be someone who didn't know her.

Lucy got out her phone and dialed. She'd kept all the notes; along with a record of what day and time they were delivered and which company delivered them. She'd learned to time and date everything because she had to cover herself with this job. Too often, there'd been problems.

For one, Lucy kept getting locked out of her email and her social media accounts and kept having to make new passwords. This slowed down her ability to do her job, and when her emails sometimes went missing, she'd started printing them out just to protect herself.

For another, there was the massage appointment she knew she'd made, but Sam, the masseuse, told her he'd never received. So he hadn't shown up and Angelica had been upset. Luckily, Lucy had been able to get Sam to come out that evening after he had finished with other clients. She'd searched her email account three times, but the email she'd sent was not in the sent folder. From then on, she'd decided not to rely on emails, but to call everything in.

Angelica had implied to Monroe that Lucy wasn't doing her job. Now Lucy noted everything and made sure she could account for every task she did for the actress if there ever came a time when she needed to. Tonight, though Monroe might blow her off, she was going to report these notes and gifts because she was concerned. It didn't seem normal, some stranger sending lingerie, and if Lucy were going to make an error, it would be to error on the side of caution.

It being evening and the dinner hour, Monroe didn't answer his phone. Likely, he was at a dinner club making deals. She left a message briefly telling him what was going on and asked him to call her.

THE NEXT MORNING as Lucy was riding in the taxi with Angelica to her salon appointment, she mentioned she'd called Monroe. Angelica shrugged it off. "People send me things all the time. You know that. You shouldn't bother Monroe with stupid stuff like this."

Lucy kept her thoughts to herself.

At the Simply Divine Beauty Shop in L.A., Lucy and Angelica stood by the reception desk waiting for the attendant to get off the phone. She hung up and then said, "Miss Glory! So good to see you! What can I do for you today?"

Lucy said, "Miss Glory is here for her nine thirty appointment."

"Oh no." The woman shook her head. "You cancelled that appointment yesterday."

"No, that's a mistake. I didn't call to cancel it." Lucy said, pulling out the email she had sent and the one she had received. "The appointment is for today at nine thirty. Hair color and nails."

"Well now, yes you did." The woman took the

salon appointment book and turned it around, placing it where they could both see it. "Yesterday at noon. See. You called and cancelled."

On the appointment calendar was clearly written: cancelled Friday, twelve ten, Lucy Wood.

"We write everything down. You called. You just don't remember."

"I did not call to cancel this appointment."

"Stupid girl." Angelica faced Lucy, furious. "Stop lying. You screwed up again. Now fix it." She marched over to the soft yellow leather couch in the reception area and sunk down onto it, waiting.

Lucy watched her march off with a sinking feeling in the pit of her stomach.

How could this be happening again? It shouldn't have, not when I've been so careful.

She turned back to the receptionist. "I don't understand how this happened. I didn't call to cancel," Lucy insisted. "Who took the call?

The receptionist raised an eyebrow and said, "I did."

"Was it a man or a woman who called?"

She gave her hard stare, and then said, "Look, this says Lucy Wood," she tapped the page three times with her long, red fingernail, "right here. It was obviously a woman."

"I …I don't understand." The whole thing had Lucy confused and frustrated as her thoughts raced.

Why would someone impersonate me and cancel the appointment? This made no sense.

"I don't understand how this happened. I didn't call." She pulled out her own appointment book and opened it. "I would have made a note if I'd called. And there's no note. It wasn't me who called."

The receptionist raised an eyebrow and gave her a look that said she clearly thought Lucy was a liar.

This was not getting them anywhere and Angelica needed her hair and her nails done.

"Can you still do her hair and nails?"

"Absolutely not. There's not enough time to do everything. She'll be lucky if we can squeeze her in for a root touch up two hours from now. You know Sebastian has a waiting list."

"Oh no. I'd hoped you could."

"Do you want to try that or not?"

"Yes, please see if we can make that happen."

"I'll be right back." The receptionist went to the back of the room and then returned with Sebastian, Angelica's hairdresser.

He walked over to where Angelica was seated. "Darling! I understand there has been a mix up. It's so hard to get good help these days. Of course, any spot that opens up is immediately taken. You know how in demand my services are. If only I'd known you were not cancelling. But this is not your fault and I'm making an exception for you today. I will skip my lunch just to fit you in and we'll take care of those roots. Will that help?"

"Sebastian," Angelica placed her hand on her heart with her usual flair of drama, "I appreciate you. My roots are a priority. Which you just know. And you are certainly right about the help." She shot Lucy a glare. "This sort of thing never happened to me before."

Lucy turned beet red, wanted to protest again that she hadn't called to cancel the appointment, but knew it would be futile. No one was listening to her or believing her.

How could this have happened?

At least they'd get Angelica in for a dye job. As far as it never happening before, maybe it hadn't, but Lucy was the fifth assistant Miss Glory had hired. Or rather, her manager, Monroe, had hired. God only knows what had happened to the first four.

"Darling, why don't you take an early lunch at Pierre's and have a glass of wine while you're waiting. They have the most divine waiter there named Avellino. I've been dying to ask him out. You ask for him and he'll take good care of you. Then when you come back, I'll restore those glorious locks of yours."

"That sounds lovely. Thank you, Sebastian."

"My pleasure, darling."

Angelica turned her attention to Lucy again. "Call them right away and get me a table."

"Yes, Miss Glory." Lucy got out her phone to look up the number of the popular L.A. restaurant. She'd be on her own for lunch, yet would still have to keep an eye on her boss. Silly as it was, they'd need two tables, one for each of them. She stepped outside to make the call so she could speak freely. "Yes. I need two tables for one, under the name Angelica Glory, both close enough to see each other."

That likely sounded ridiculous, but a table where she could keep an eye on her boss was what Lucy needed. Angelica with two hours to do nothing but drink wine and wait for an appointment could spell trouble if her drinking got out of hand in public. This wasn't a good start to the day.

In the taxi on the way to lunch, Angelica said, "I was embarrassed. And I do not like having to beg. Pay heed. This isn't the first mistake you've made. One more incident like today and you're fired."

"It won't happen again."

With no idea how it happened this time, Lucy couldn't be sure of that, but she did know she was competent at her job and gave it her best. This wasn't a screw up she would have made. Unfortunately, these strange things that she could have sworn she didn't do just kept happening.

Why did this kind of thing keep happening? Why would somebody call the salon and pretend to be me? Are they trying to get me fired? And if so, who?

She couldn't imagine who. Her head was already starting to hurt. This was a bad start to what would be a very long day.

BY THE END of the day, Lucy was exhausted and had just kicked off her shoes to rest on the couch after putting a small frozen lasagna in the oven when her phone rang.

Monroe's name flashed on the screen.

"Hello, Monroe. Thank you for calling me back."

"Do you still have the notes?"

"Yes. I keep and file everything she receives."

"Good. I want to see them."

"They're at the office."

"Meet me there in an hour."

"Okay."

They hung up and Lucy put the phone down with a sigh, and then went in the kitchen to turn off the oven.

There was just enough time for a quick shower and to make a peanut butter and jelly sandwich before she had to go out again to make it through L.A. traffic to be at the office in an hour. Eating a sandwich as she drove wasn't how she'd wanted to end her day, though it did keep the pounds off not having time for regular meals. She really needed a raise. And a day, or better yet, a week off.

By the time she'd made it back to her apartment and had fallen into bed, she was glad she'd made the call to Monroe. He'd taken it seriously and, after seeing the notes side by side he'd made three calls. The first was to the head of a company who advised on security threats such as stalking, the second to a colleague whose client had been shot by a love-crazed fan, and the third to a bodyguard service based in Montana, which came recommended by the colleague. He was taking no chances with his famous client. Now, everything was arranged.

Angelica and Lucy would be flying to Montana to lay low, and a bodyguard service had been hired to protect the actress.

Lucy's wish had partially been granted. Overtime pay and a vacation. A vacation, which included spending twenty-four-seven with Angelica. And they were leaving in three days.

Luckily, Monroe was informing Angelica of all this. Lucy had tomorrow off to finalize anything she needed to before she went out of town and to prepare for the trip, while also clearing everything on Angelica's calendar. Not really a day off, but it was better than none.

The following day, she'd be helping Angelica pack. Angelica would have to get her nails done somewhere other than her favorite salon in L.A., if they couldn't squeeze her in before they flew out. After the way the receptionist reacted to Lucy, she doubted she'd have luck when she called in the morning to ask them to squeeze Angelica in again.

She couldn't even tell them why Angelica was leaving.

Monroe didn't want the tabloids to pick up the story. The official spiel was Miss Glory was taking a much-needed vacation at a spa.

Lucy couldn't tell a soul what was really going on. She shivered. Someone was stalking Angelica.

I hope and pray that one day domestic abuse will no longer take place anywhere. Until that day . . . Please know that if this has happened to you, you are not alone and you are loved. Reach out to someone, anyone, and let one of us help. – Debra Parmley, founder Shimmy Mob Memphis.

United States International Domestic Abuse Hotline
1-800-799-SAFE (7233), or 1-800-787-3224 (TTY)

For more information about domestic abuse, resources and information about international Shimmy Mob go to

www.ShimmyMob.com

ABOUT DEBRA PARMLEY

"Every day we are alive is a beautiful day." – Debra Parmley

Debra Parmley is a multi genre, hybrid romance author born in Columbus, Ohio and raised in Springfield, Ohio. She has lived just outside Memphis, Tennessee since 1997. Debra attended Marywood University in Scranton, Pennsylvania and was the first student to win first place in two categories of the Delta Epsilon Sigma Beta Epsilon Chapter writing competition, in create prose and in informal expository. Her poetry was published in literary journals while attending college. She holds a BA in English Literature.

Debra enjoys spreading love, one story at a time. Fascinated by fairy tales and folktales ever since she was young, she always ends her stories with a happy ever after. Damsels in distress stories favorites, and you'll find this theme in many of her stories. An Air Force veteran's wife, Debra enjoys writing military romance. Veterans hold a special place in her heart.

Debra has set foot in over thirteen countries. Her books often include elements from her travels. Her three favorite things are dark chocolate, visiting the beach and ocean, and hearing from her readers. Each card, and letter is a treasured gift, like finding a perfect shell upon the beach.

Visit debraparmley.com

ORIGINAL BROTHERHOOD
PROTECTORS SERIES

BY ELLE JAMES

Brotherhood Protectors Series

Montana SEAL (#1)

Bride Protector SEAL (#2)

Montana D-Force (#3)

Cowboy D-Force (#4)

Montana Ranger (#5)

Montana Dog Soldier (#6)

Montana SEAL Daddy (#7)

Montana Ranger's Wedding Vow (#8)

Montana SEAL Undercover Daddy (#9)

Cape Cod SEAL Rescue (#10)

Montana SEAL Friendly Fire (#11)

Montana SEAL's Mail-Order Bride (#12)

Montana Rescue (Sleeper SEAL)

Hot SEAL Salty Dog (SEALs in Paradise)

Brotherhood Protectors Vol 1

ABOUT ELLE JAMES

ELLE JAMES also writing as MYLA JACKSON is a *New York Times* and *USA Today* Bestselling author of books including cowboys, intrigues and paranormal adventures that keep her readers on the edges of their seats. With over eighty works in a variety of sub-genres and lengths she has published with Harlequin, Samhain, Ellora's Cave, Kensington, Cleis Press, and Avon. When she's not at her computer, she's traveling, snow skiing, boating, or riding her ATV, dreaming up new stories. Learn more about Elle James at www.elle-james.com

Website | Facebook | Twitter | GoodReads | Newsletter | BookBub | Amazon

Follow Elle!
www.ellejames.com
ellejames@ellejames.com

facebook.com/ellejamesauthor

twitter.com/ElleJamesAuthor